LILY MABURA is current⌐
American University of Si.⌐⌐
Jomo Kenyatta Prize for Literature, Kenya's National ʙᴏᴏᴋ ᴡᴇᴇᴋ
Literary Award and the Ellen Meloy Desert Writers Award. Her
short story, 'How Shall We Kill the Bishop?', was shortlisted for the
2010 Caine Prize for African Writing. Her publications include a
first novel titled *The Pretoria Conspiracy* and four children's books:
Oma, Saleh Kanta and the Cavaliers, Seth the Silly Gorilla and *Ali the
Little Sultan.*

LILY MABURA

HOW SHALL WE KILL THE BISHOP?

AND OTHER STORIES

Pearson Education Limited is a company incorporated in England and Wales, having its registered office at Edinburgh Gate, Harlow, Essex, CM20 2JE. Registered company number: 872828

www.africanwriters.com

Text © Lily Mabura 2012

This collection first published in 2012 by Pearson Education Ltd

'How Shall We Kill the Bishop?' appeared in *Wasafiri: The Magazine of International Contemporary Writing* (Routledge) 23.53 (Spring 2008): 6–9; anthologised in *A Life in Full and Other Stories: The Caine Prize for African Writing 2010*; 'Elgon' appeared in *Callaloo* (Johns Hopkins UP) 30.2 (2007): 527–32; 'Man in Ultramarine Pyjamas' appeared in *The Fish Anthology 2007* (Fish Publishing, Ireland): 178–85; 'Up on the Hill' appeared in PRISM *international* (University of British Columbia, Canada) 43.2 (2005): 19–29. 'Leaving Lamu' appeared in *Imagining Ourselves Website – International Museum for Women* (2006); 'Sweet Sugarcane Secrets' appeared in *Timbuktu – The International Arts and Literary Journal Made in Wales Website* (June 2005); 'The Boskopman' appeared in *Pacific Northwest Inlanders Online* (2004); 'Our Lady of Lourdes 16th Annual Knights of Columbus Spaghetti Dinner' appeared in G21 – *The World's Magazine Website* (July 2003).

16 15 14 13 12
IMP 10 9 8 7 6 5 4 3 2 1

British Library Cataloguing in Publication Data
A catalogue record for this book is available from the British Library.

ISBN 978 0 435075 41 5

Typeset by Sara Rafferty
Cover artwork © Eva Mabura
Author photograph © Lily Mabura
Printed by Multivista Global Ltd

Acknowledgements
Every effort has been made to contact copyright holders of material reproduced in this book. Any omissions will be rectified in subsequent printings if notice is given to the publishers.

CONTENTS

ACKNOWLEDGEMENTS

I wish to acknowledge the inspiring support of my MFA in Creative Writing thesis committee at the University of Idaho, which included professors Kim Barnes, Mary C. Blew and Richard Reardon. My thanks also go to professors Gary Williams and Mary Ann Judge. I have fond memories of you all. To my doctoral Creative Writing and Theatre professors at the University of Missouri-Columbia—Trudy Lewis, Marly Swick and Heather Carver—thank you for your support and guidance.

I also wish to acknowledge financial support, in the form of international fellowships and travel awards, from the American Association of University Women (AAUW), P.E.O. International and the Ellen Meloy Fund for Desert Writers.

In addition, I wish to acknowledge the following journals and websites in which earlier versions of some of the stories in this collection first appeared: 'Man in Ultramarine Pyjamas' in the July 2007 *Fish Anthology*, Ireland; 'How Shall We Kill the Bishop?' a finalist in Glimmer Train's Fiction Open 2006/2007 and *Wasafiri: The Magazine of International Contemporary Writing*, UK; 'Up on the Hill' in PRISM *international*; 'Leaving Lamu' in the 2006 Imagining Ourselves website, International Museum for Women; 'Elgon' in *Callaloo*; 'Sweet Sugarcane Secrets' in *Timbuktu—The International Arts and Literary Journal Made in Wales* website; 'The Boskopman' in the *Pacific Northwest Inlanders Online*; and 'Our Lady of Lourdes 16th Annual Knights of Columbus Spaghetti Dinner' in *G21—The World's Magazine* website.

To Eva Mabura: thank you for your sisterly motivation; you suggested that I title the lead story with a question posed in the narrative, 'How Shall We Kill the Bishop?' Last, and not in any way least, I treasure the love and support of all my family, friends and Pearson's publishing team, among them Lynette Lisk.

Dedication
For my family and friends

MAN IN ULTRAMARINE PYJAMAS

There is this man that I know. Perhaps I should take that back and say that he is a man you can only know from what you hear because he talks to no one. I think that he has always been at the back of my mind, pieces of him gradually coalescing into a mass of connective tissue that could be said to be a semblance of him. I have heard countless stories about him from my mother. These are stories she did not really intend to tell for she is not the gossipy kind. I have also been watching him for years, from way back. My father occupied this studio then. He had it brimming with charcoal drawings and sculptures, some of which my mother has since done away with. I would sit by this window as he worked and look down into this man's yard.

I wish I could tell you his name, but I have a feeling that would spoil everything. My aim is not to embarrass him; I merely wish to paint him. The thought has often occurred to me, but never the opportune moment; not one like this. This is the first time I am seeing him asleep with his head against the driver's seat of his car, face up, rather than slumped down onto the steering wheel. There is always something tragic and desperate about him in that pose. He reminds me of Van Gogh's *Old Man with His Head in His Hands.*

There is no veil of drunkenness on his face this morning, no bleary nostrils, no streak of white saliva on a gaping jaw. Plus he is in pyjamas I have never seen him in before—ultramarine pyjamas he probably has not worn for years. You can tell that a good tailor had taken his time on them. A good tailor is hard to find in Kericho because this is Kenya's tea capital. It is hilly and it is green and it rains as it pleases. Yes, he must have gotten his ultramarine pyjamas elsewhere. I shift my weight from one foot to the other. He must have forfeited his ritualistic, alcohol-induced

1

passing out last night, I tell myself. He had arrived home, I imagine, at whatever time of the night, had his supper or perhaps not, but from his clean state obviously had taken a bath, had next gotten into these ultramarine pyjamas, walked out of his house, opened the door to his car, pushed back the driver's seat, and then lay there till this bright and early morning.

It's a quiet morning that gives the impression that there isn't another soul awake for miles. The sun's rays, coming from an odd angle through the sycamore trees, stand between him and me. Some leaves sparkle like green marble as the rays touch them and are then reflected away. The sun manages to filter through others, turning them into sheer, greenish yellow screens. On any other morning I would have gladly painted it for you, this expansive palette of Chrysolite with flickering cast shadows from dry, dark twigs. You'd see it as I see it, interlaced with lengths of cobweb that are only visible at this time of the day when the angling of the light has them glistening like hairline rainbows. But there he is and I worry that he might awaken, that the light might change, that there might never be such a moment again. It is as Monet said: colour, any colour, lasts a second, sometimes three or four minutes at a time. What to do, what to paint in three or four minutes, he had asked.

His face, I finally decide; it's the best place to begin. The rest I am likely to see again, tomorrow perhaps, the day after that … I sketch him on a canvas I have been reserving for a landscape. I woke up with the intention of painting outside today, in the tea estates where I might find pickers doing their job in silence. But his face compels me now, and I decide to do the painting in oils even though they are hard to work with a knife and take forever to dry. They can take months. But it is the effect I am after. I like to think of a drying oil painting as a fermenting tea: the colour and the aroma all depend on it.

I start with a pale hue of raw sienna mixed with linseed oil

2

for an under layer. Painting under layers always gives me time to think, reconsider my subject. To truly capture a face, my father used to say, you had to take into account what had happened to it before. You had to think time and people. Time for this man is, well, a lot; at least when you compare his age with that of the men in my family. My brother died at twenty-seven while serving on the Kenyan UN Protection Force in Bosnia. He was on foot patrol near Brezani, a commune of Srebrenica, and tripped on a step mine. My father had died two years earlier of pneumonia. My mother said it was because he liked walking in the rain and would not be bothered with carrying an umbrella or putting on a raincoat. Kericho, he used to say, has been raining every afternoon from the beginning of time. He was of the opinion that there was nothing one could do to keep from getting wet.

He is sixty, this man, like my own father would have been if he were alive. In that regard it is interesting watching him. I imagine certain parts of my father—a patch of skin maybe, some grey hairs, that slowed gait perhaps—would look like his. A stroke from two years back has deepened and fossilised the lines in his face, and sometimes I perceive a shadow leisurely emerging from underneath. It is a stormy brown, like you would get by mixing scarlet vermilion and emerald green; stormy brown over the under layer, I think, and on that thin glazes of terra rosa.

My mother does not like the shape of his head. It is as oblong as an African pumpkin, she asserts, and admonishes me to be wary of men with such heads. They have no luck when it comes to love, she is convinced. Her conviction, of course, is not only drawn from this one man alone. You understand that I cannot divulge specific names, but I will point you in the general direction: there is that man who works for the Kericho Wagon Works (they no longer make wagons; it's just the original name); the one who insists on shaking everyone's hand after Mass; and the handsome waiter at the historic Tea Hotel. *All* ill-fated when it comes to love, she will point out, dead certain; it is as though she has a mental list of such men that progresses on to the infinitesimal.

Personally, I think her repulsive obsession for heads began when she met my father. I recall one year when he took a trip to Paris on an exhibition tour. He sent her a postcard of the martyr St Denis standing in Notre Dame, his severed head in his hands. She threw away the postcard without bothering to read it. If my father was particularly taken by your head, he would carve it. I remember the studio being filled with them while growing up, shelf after shelf: the head of Puran Singh Ji—that Sikh saint who had spent almost five decades in Kericho; the head of Vick Preston—for his Safari Rally exploits; the head of a Nairobi beggar; the head of a tired tea picker; my mother's head; my brother's head; my own. She did away with them when he died. I only managed to save my head and that of my brother. I remember that he called that day, my brother. I was downstairs and my mother was up here, taking them down from the shelves one by one. 'Let's not talk about heads, Leslie,' he had said. 'I am in Srebrenica.'

From Srebrenica we got some of his personal items, his medals, his spare blue UN beret, and a small notebook in which he meticulously recorded each day's events. These items lie on his bed in his room. My mother has never read the notebook. I read through the first page, but never got to the second. It no longer matters who has done what in Srebrenica, he had written; what you should know is this: Kristina Lazić, blind and mentally ill, was burned in her house; Vidoje Pavle was crucified and burned; Andjelko Mladjenović was caught off guard while working with his mother and his head was cut off; Aleska Perić's throat was slit and the letter 'U' carved on his chest; Stojan Stevanović was found beaten, stabbed and castrated, his penis in his mouth; Radjoko Milošević was burned in his house while celebrating St George's Day; Soka Vujić was killed with a pitchfork; one boy, I am still trying to establish his name, was found with his tongue and

4

ears cut off and a cross carved on his forehead as if to atone for Aleska Perić and anyone else who might have had the 'U' carved on them by the Ustashi.

Is Srebrenica ever like this in the morning? Can you find, in Srebrenica, a man and a car who have had the chance to grow as old as this? This man's car is a 1978 Ford. To stop it from rusting away, he had it set by the chassis on ballast rocks. I can't imagine how many miles he put on that car, my mother says. It was not uncommon, some years back, to see him impatiently following a tea truck through the narrow roads of the estates and then speeding off once they reached the open tarmac roads. She was a brilliant chrome yellow then, the Ford. When he drove past you in that car, mother says, he was a comet flashing across the evening sky—a fireball.

He was courting a woman in Nairobi, it was said. If he had the time to make it to the city and back, he would go. There wasn't an extra minute that he spent at the Brook Bond Tea Company where he worked as a junior manager. According to my mother—she works as tea taster in the same company—he squandered all his chances for promotion and never rose from the starting position he had been hired for. Some people, she says, thought he was possessed, others thought he was battling unrequited love, others made wild guesses. The truth was nobody knew for sure.

The only things certain are that he suddenly parked the Ford and would not steer her onto the high road again. He married too—as suddenly as he had parked the Ford. She was a migrant tea picker. Father thought she was beautiful and carved her head. He could never carve this man's head though. He's not made to be sculptured, Leslie, he would say; painted perhaps, and with a persistent doubt in one's choice of colours. A hammer and a chisel are too definite. Much too definite, I tell you.

I like his lips; they are as dark as chocolate and firmly edged. I botched mine with lipstick. I got an allergic reaction that spotted

5

what had once been a uniform umber. Now I am afraid the man I will love might look at them and think—Oh, whatever did she do to them? A tap of water runs downstairs. It's mother making ready to brew some tea. I sweep the Ford's outline with the most brilliant chrome yellow. What colour was she on the high road, a man in love at her wheel? Granted, the actual colour of the car has faded from its former glory, but I cannot help thinking of it as a comet: flaming yellow, spurting yellow, a tail end of yellows not to be seen again from Planet Earth for hundreds of years. Chrome yellow, yes, but maybe also, cadmium, Naples …

I hear my mother on the wooden stairs. She halts a stair or two away from the studio's door. I imagine her hand on the hand-carved railing father made. She likes touching the things that he made. Sometimes she walks about the house, arms outstretched, running them over this sculpture or that; the wooden fruit bowl he gave her on their last anniversary; a favourite picture frame; sometimes their bedroom door, which has an elaborate Zanzibari motif on it. 'You know that you cannot come in,' I say.

'Oh, yes,' she sighs. 'Your father used to say that too. I have the basilisk look, you think?'

'Mama … I'll show it to you when I'm done.'

'The smell of the linseed woke me up. It's been ages since you used it. What's the hurry?'

'No hurry.'

'Well,' she says, 'you have a phone call.'

I open the door: 'Who from?'

She looks down at the palette in my hand. 'Ultramarine … Are you painting a saint's robes?'

I raise my eyebrows. I have my look on, I suppose. My brother claimed that I often used it to usurp my parents' authority. You are the product of their unbridled premarital passion, he used to say, and that makes them reluctant disciplinarians as far as you're concerned.

6

'Some gallery,' she says.

I step out of the studio, painting knife in one hand, palette in the other, and push the door shut with the bare heel of my foot. My mother chuckles softly and then turns around. I follow her down the stairs, staring at her thin straight back beneath the crumpled white sleeping shirt and the gray-streaked pile of plaits on her head. She assesses people, I feel, like she assesses teas. If you watch her keenly with a person she has just met you will notice how she subtly inclines her long nose to their skin. She inhales people and judges them by their flavour. She swirls their words in her brain, atomising them, allowing them to linger about until she is certain of their character. The man in ultramarine pyjamas, she once told me, used to smell of lime blossoms and mimosa. And that was when he had the Ford on the high road. He had a different smell at the end: that of a very large hospital.

I pick up the phone. It's Neil from Gallery Watatu. 'You're one painting short,' he says.

'And what difference does one painting make?'

'Leslie Kering,' he says, with long vowels. 'You can't exhibit this way. The rules say at least ten pieces for a solo exhibition. You have nine. Send me one more.'

'It's not done.'

'Finish it today and send it to me tomorrow.'

'It will not be dry tomorrow.'

'You have done it in oils.'

'Yes.'

'Well, then, use your imagination. Let me hear you say: "I will send it tomorrow, Neil."'

'I will send it tomorrow, Neil,' I repeat.

'Leslie—' he says.

'Yes?'

He pauses awhile. I hear something I do not recognise in his brief silence. It's been six months since I was in Nairobi, six

7

months since I last saw him, six months since I painted anything of significance.

'Send it,' he says and then hangs up.

I turn around and find my mother watching me. She is slowly grinding dry green tea leaves between the palms of her hands and letting them fall into an open kettle of boiling water. She makes wonderful aromatic green teas this way. When not at work, she can spend a whole day steaming the green buds and drying them out in the oven. Her mother was a tea taster and reared her to be a tea taster. The tea farm she inherited took second place to tea tasting. It was too much work, so she had rented it out but for a few bushes of her own, which she picks and processes herself. I love tea, but in a different way from my mother. There is absolutely no distance between it and her. My brother loved tea as she loves it. He matched her passion. Before he left for Bosnia she gave him two tins of tea and his very own copy of the *Kissa Yojoki*—Book of Tea.

'You could send it by train,' she says. 'The containers aren't always full.'

'Yes,' I say, bounding up the stairs. 'I suppose I could.'

He's still there, asleep in the Ford. I am ready to do his pyjamas now. Ultramarine for a man in ultramarine pyjamas—am I painting a saint's robes? I dip the knife into the paint and touch it onto the canvas. I know I can finish it today, but how to get it to Neil without smudging and dust heaping upon it? It's not the Kericho dust I am worried about for there is hardly any, it is the dust that might be inside the train and in Nairobi where Neil will be waiting. Should I use one of the wooden crates my father used to transport his sculptures in? I could seal the interior with nylon sheets and nail the painting to one side. It would work, wouldn't it?

She appears suddenly in the yard below—the man's wife. From the way she is dressed you can tell she is headed out to the tea estates. She has a large-rimmed papyrus hat on to help shade her face from the sun and the rain. A plastic overcoat hangs from her shoulders to protect her clothes as she pushes through the narrow paths between the rows of tea. Like all pickers, she wears gumboots. They are simple black gumboots you'd find in any *duka* in Kericho. You need to wear them with socks else they'll rub your calves sore. They are a good precaution against any snakes in the tea. Thus apparelled, she stands staring at him asleep in that Ford.

How to describe her? She is like a bird with a destroyed nest. The tea flushes all year; all year she waits for these early mornings so that she can head out to it. She does not return until evening when the sun has gone down completely and dew has started forming on the bushes she has been harvesting all day long. This is her life. I wonder if she sees it this way or I merely imagine it to be so. She stares at him for a long time. It's as though she has never seen him in the ultramarine pyjamas either.

Suddenly, she looks up at the window, at me, and I step back. I do not know why I step back. When I look out of the window again she is gone and the man is still asleep. I am wondering how long he will sleep when the doorbell rings. Something tells me it is her. What does she want? She, like her husband, talks to no one, never sets foot in anyone else's house. I put my knife and palette down and walk down the stairs: it *is* her. She is with my mother on the front porch. The door is shut, but I can see them both through the glass.

They are talking with their tall backs to me. The man's wife folds her arms across her chest, and my mother folds her arms across her chest. Those arms look like tea stalks. Cut them down to the very ground and they will grow back. It is when they go down the porch steps together, they do not turn back to the house, that I immediately know in my heart what my eyes later confirm from the studio's window.

9

They walk to the man in ultramarine pyjamas, both of them, and stand there staring at him. The man's wife has a white piece of cloth in her arms now. She opens it up. It is a large bed sheet. She holds one end, and my mother holds the other end. Together, they drape it over the dead man and his car.

I step away from the window and stare at the painting: his ultramarine pyjamas are only halfway done. It would be reasonable to try to finish them, from memory, but I find I cannot. I get out of the studio and down the stairs to the basement where my father's crates are still stacked up like unused coffins. I pick one that will do and prepare it for the painting. I am done by midday but cannot get it out of the basement until someone from the factory swings by to inquire after my mother. I explain what has happened. This man who has come to inquire after my mother nods. He is a tea taster like her. I watch his nose involuntarily twitch in the wind as I ask if he could help with the crate. He nods again and we load the crate onto the back of my father's old truck.

It is raining by the time I return from the train station. When I look out of the studio window, the man in ultramarine pyjamas, his yellow Ford, and the white sheet are all gone. Even the ballast rocks, which have supported the yellow Ford for years, are gone. All that remains of their previous existence is a rectangular patch of bare ground muddying under the rain.

I make dinner and eat it alone because mother does not return home. She is helping out with the guests next door. They come and go, these guests, despite this man and his wife who never talked to them. That night I sleep in my brother's bed, his black leather-bound notebook in my hand. When I wake up in the morning I find the door to the bedroom open and a warm kettle of tea sitting on the stove in the kitchen. Mother has been here, but is no longer here. Came and went. I sit at the kitchen table and pour myself a cup of tea. Because I like it with honey, I pour some in. Then I open my brother's notebook and begin reading from the second page: today, he writes, the Church of the Holy Archangel Michael was blown up.

You want to know whether I continued and read it all, I imagine. Yes, I did—all day long and the next. I even read his letters, all sealed in envelopes and addressed to me and mother, but never mailed. Now, after reading everything, I spend endless days in bed. My mind churns the word Srebrenica. It swirls in there like a drum of paints that might never homogenise. Srebrenica, Srebrenica, Srebrenica …

When Neil calls, I do not know what day it is. What time of day it is. I only know it is in the afternoon because it is raining. 'I have sold it,' he cries.

'Sold what?' I ask.

'Your incomplete man in ultramarine pyjamas,' he replies, ecstatic.

Are they going to bury him in his ultramarine pyjamas, I wonder.

'Leslie,' Neil says, 'I am here … at the Tea Hotel.'

He is here, at the Tea Hotel. I consider that for a little while. 'I'll be over shortly,' I tell him.

I walk up the stairs to my studio and open the door. The air has aged and is now stale. The palette is caked with dry paint. From the shelf I pick my head, the one father carved. I leave it on the kitchen table before walking out of the house. There is a note taped to it, for mother, for whatever time she comes home today. *Will be back soon*, it says, followed by *I shall work even harder than I do now*. Yes, the last part of the sentence is Vincent's. The one thing Vincent has taught me is to patiently consider everything: light, words … yes, even death. Death lay there under the sun just a few days ago. Luxuriating. He was wearing ultramarine pyjamas and riding a yellow Ford and had let me consider him.

11

HOW SHALL WE KILL THE BISHOP?

It was Fr Yasin Lordman who had asked the question—nothing more than a joke. A most inappropriate joke since he loved the bishop. It was Easter besides. But the three other priests in the vicarage heard him. Dafala, the cook who had set a breakfast in keeping with Holy Saturday, heard him. Perhaps it was the weak kettle of black sugarless tea that was to blame, or the sleep raging in his mind, or the pain in his knees for bearing his weight all night, or his fellow priests who would not join him for their usual morning cigarette.

'I'm fasting cigarettes today,' the youngest priest, Fr Ahmed, had declared. He had been ordained at the beginning of the year and had been trying to quit smoking since.

'The bishop would want us to,' Fr Seif had said. He smoked more for the company than anything else.

'He is ill and he is watching us, Yasin. What do you think he says to the Archbishop in Nairobi, to the Nuncio, to Rome?' Fr Dugo had asked.

'He is the problem, then, I suppose,' Fr Yasin had said. 'Tell me, how shall we rid ourselves of him? How shall we kill the bishop?'

The three were now staring at him under the flickering light of a candle, which was set at the middle of the dining table. The generator had been shut down on Maundy Thursday and the vicarage stood dark and pensive like the arid land surrounding it. 'You should whip yourself,' Fr Dugo said.

Fr Yasin rose from the table and walked into the kitchen. Dafala retrieved the bishop's breakfast tray from the wood oven. Dafala was almost as old as the bishop. In his lengthy white *kanzu*, regularly mistaken for a priest's frock, he was no less of a priest than any of them. His life was single-mindedly devoted

12

to the vicarage. He had no property that he could call his own. He was celibate. He was a man who had lived out his priesthood unwittingly, Fr Yasin thought. With his conscientious hands, Dafala now covered the bishop's scone and scrambled eggs with a purple crocheted napkin. Next to them he placed a flask of tea and chinaware. Then a small glass vase, often used in the chapel, with a single purple rose stem. Dafala had roses for all occasions and kept a kitchen garden even in the worst of droughts. He skimped on everybody's drinking water if he had to. He handed the tray to Fr Yasin without a word.

Fr Yasin knocked on the bishop's door twice before entering. The knock was perfunctory. The bishop was knelt on a prie-dieu at one end of his room. There the wall jutted out like an apse and served as his own private chapel. He was awake and fully dressed as usual. His bed was made even though he had taken to returning to it by mid-morning. Fr Yasin had begun judging his daily disposition by the length of his random siestas. The bishop's broad back was to him and he stared at it under the smoky yellow light of the candelabrum burning on his desk. It was a back still unbent by age or illness, and his neck rose from it like a ship's mast. Above his white shirt collar was the familiar edge of his hairline from which it was so easy to see a clear throbbing vein under the sun. He was always the last man to break into a sweat on the hockey pitch. He looked very much his old self from the back, but his face had begun to change—it resembled his father's more and more each day, Fr Yasin thought.

There was a photo of the bishop's father on his desk. Having one made a difference, Fr Yasin had always felt. It was the only thing he envied in other men. Perhaps that was the reason he loved this photo. Raji Lal Sandhu stood there beside his Kenyan wife in his white turban and generous Sikh moustache. He had the face of a man who had worked hard his entire life; a man who, in exchange for a piece of land that he could call his own, had left the Sikh units of the Indian Colonial Army for the ballast pits feeding the construction of the Kenya–Uganda railway. Every time Fr Yasin looked at this photo, he noticed something new. Holding the bishop's breakfast tray that morning, for instance, he noticed that here was a man who had determined to forget India.

It was the condition of man he was inclined to think. Fr Ahmed, for example, was hard bent on forgetting cigarettes; Fr Seif, in his determination to forget the woman he loved, intruded on everyone's quiet time because he could not stand his own; Fr Dugo determined to forget that the bishop had tested him most before admission; and Dafala determined to forget that the bishop was sick at all and carried on as usual. If the bishop ever determined to forget anything, though, it was sealed in his heart, well hidden beneath the surface of his face.

That face was now cast upwards, to the crucifix nailed onto the innermost recess of the apse. This was the only crucifix still standing in the vicarage. The rest had all been taken down and replaced with bare wooden crosses the evening before. The bishop's crucifix, however, was still standing: Christ's head like a drooping flower, his cranium a framework of metal petals crowned with barbed wire; his cheekbones high and pointed above the hollow flesh; his nose a sharp edge of metal; his beard an emerald mixture of rust and solder; his splayed hands broken at the joints, with ragged strips for fingers; his chest the very semblance of a fallen warrior's breastplate—severely punished and bloodied; below that a gaping hole, as jagged as a cave's mouth, exposing a metal vertebrae blackened with soot; his penis a small and humble-looking rod of metal, placed at an odd angle, as though the sculptor had considered leaving it out all together and then, upon further pondering the matter, had realized that it could hardly be ignored, that it would be more visible in its absence than actuality; and his legs, of course, those corroded buttresses that still held up the church long after Golgotha.

'Fr Yasin.'

'Your Grace?'

'Have breakfast with me,' the bishop said, rising from his knees. There was a faint smile on his thin face. 'And what has Dafala made this morning?'

Fr Yasin placed the breakfast tray on a table facing the patio and lifted the purple napkin.

'Hmmm. There is no cook like Dafala, don't you agree, Yasin?' he asked. 'In his mind's handbook is an explicit set of rules on how to cook for a sick priest, a disobedient priest, a vain priest, a good priest ...'

Fr Yasin laughed and pulled him a chair.

'How is his garden faring?'

'Well, let's say that the birds will have none of it and neither will the locusts if they come this year. They would need pliers for teeth from the way he's been working the wire mesh.'

The bishop chuckled, but his brown eyes seemed tired and somewhat sunken, like a drying riverbed slowly shrinking away from its banks.

'He'd rather be telling you this himself, of course,' Fr Yasin said. He opened the flask and poured the bishop a cup of tea. 'He's not used to having someone else bring in your breakfast.'

The bishop sipped his tea and said nothing. He was weaning Dafala from himself, Fr Yasin suspected. When he had been posted to this Kenyan northern frontier town thirty years ago, he had come with two things: his mule and Dafala. A young pregnant Borana prostitute, groaning with labour pangs, had stumbled into their camp the very first morning. The bishop had carried her to his sleeping bag, Dafala had boiled some hot water, and Yasin Lordman had been born. He had a mulatto skin for which the only logical explanation out here was a white soldier from the British military training base. The base was a remnant of the colonial legacy standing among stunted Acacia trees and withered

15

shrubs of Solanum. The stunts of sparse grass surrounding the base were too brittle for cattle to graze on—too brittle even for the camels. There were no Doum palms close by either, and Dafala always explained this by stating that sacred plants could not flourish near the base.

When Fr Yasin stepped into the patio and lit his cigarette, he could see the old military base with its floodlights beaming out towards the rising sun, which burned dark purple and red, its brow on the dunned horizon as yellow as ostrich yolk. With time, additional military bases had cropped up, government bases that periodically filled with local troops. They were like Roman garrisons, ever sending out legions through this gateway town into the troubled desert beyond. Rumour had it that there was a huge battalion on the way. It was the talk of the town, a distraction from the sick dogs that would not stop howling, from the dry animal carcasses in the bush, and watering holes caked with mud. He should have informed the bishop, but there was no need to tell him right away. He had enough to worry about with the emptying school, falling church attendance, and the overcrowded hospital. Fr Yasin wanted him to enjoy his breakfast. If the battalion was arriving today, he would hear it.

The bishop joined him on the patio, a cup of tea in one hand. 'The Lord should give us peace for he has given us all else, Yasin. It was what Augustine prayed for at the end.'

What Augustine had actually prayed for, Fr Yasin thought, and what the bishop was perhaps praying for, was what Augustine had penned after those words—the peace that is repose, the peace of the Sabbath, and the peace that knows no evening. One hardly forgot Augustine, Fr Yasin felt; not if you read him with passion and plenty of time on your hands like he had while on a pre-ordination retreat at the Red Sea port of Massawa. The heat in Massawa was as exhausting as it was here, as exhausting as it must have been for Augustine farther along that North African shoreline. Sometimes days would go by with hardly a breeze finding its way over the water. At such times red algae would appear suddenly and bloom endlessly, miles and miles of it, as if from the very Suez to the Strait of Bab al Mandeb, like streaks of thick camel blood that would not dissolve away. Then it would die, unexpectedly, and the sea would turn from red to rusty. Eventually Fr Yasin would wake up one morning and find the algae gone altogether, the sea blue-green again.

That was how droughts ended here: when you least expected—out of the blue. You simply awoke one morning to the sound of rainfall. The grass, like it always did, would have budded overnight and the women, who always showed up at sunrise for maize rations, indeed, who were already at the gates, would show up as usual, but with their long hair wet, their clothes dripping wet, their faces already nourished.

'The need to confess overwhelms me today, Father,' the bishop said.

His words startled Fr Yasin, and he looked away in embarrassment, unprepared for such access to the bishop's heart even though he had been contemplating it only a moment ago. 'I'm hardly the man for it, Your Grace,' he said. 'I could place a call to the Nuncio, if you like. He's your old friend. He knows you best.'

The bishop remained silent for a while, gazing at the sunrise. 'I cannot speak to Felice right now, but I have a letter for him. There, on my desk. Mail it for me.'

By its weight, Fr Yasin could tell on his way to his room, it was several pages long. He was going to mail it later in the day when the post office opened. There was no hurry. Sometimes it took almost a month for a letter to reach Nairobi. Dafala had poured half a pail of water into the washbasin. He used it to shave and bathe. Then he lay on his bed and slept.

The rumble of diesel engines and the laboured rotation

of crankshafts woke him up. The air was already tinged with the smell of dust, hot rubber, and exhausted clutches. It was the battalion slowly pouring in. Soldiers' voices and soldiers' hard combat boots, hitting the dry sandy ground in unbroken descent, could be heard alongside the rolling machinery.

When Fr Yasin emerged from the vicarage, there were soldiers everywhere, milling about in desert camouflage fatigues and standard-issue rifles. The town, generally sleepy and desolate, was now an anthill of tough unfamiliar faces from other provinces. Fr Yasin made his way towards the post office slowly, the bishop's letter in his shirt pocket, the smell of soldiers' sweat in his nose, as old and as rank as a nomad's. He was standing at the doors of the post office when he saw the altar girl, Salima, across the street. Their regular set of altar boys had left town with their families when the drought had begun in search of more reliable waterholes for their livestock; they were deep in the sun scorched land where wars were fought over whatever little water and pasture remained. Salima had landed their job inadvertently when she had scaled the vicarage's walls and Fr Ahmed, taking an early evening walk, had spied her in Dafala's garden. It had taken two mad dashes around the vicarage for him to corner her. Her penance, it was decided, was to serve as an altar girl and join the priests every Sunday afternoon in the chapel where they practised the hymn 'Salve Festa Dies' in preparation for Holy Saturday. It was Fr Dugo who had come up with the idea—to surprise the bishop. Without the altar boys their in-house choir had somewhat diminished in strength not to mention that they were sorely lacking in the alto department. Salima was the panacea. Such was the strength of her soprano! It was amazing that it could be found in so scrawny a creature. Added onto that was the fact that she had memorised the entire Gregorian melody, in Latin no less, during the first practice while they, to learn it, had been listening to a taped version the entire Lent. For her prodigious memory, they had dabbed her Giordano Bruno.

Salima, however, had not shown up for the last choir practice. Fr Ahmed was convinced that her family had moved. Fr Seif differed and revealed that he had sent her home with excess rations every time she had shown up for practice. Fr Dugo, distrusting the exact excessiveness of Fr Seif's rations, had told him off. Fr Yasin thought that they were all unnecessarily worried, but did not have adequate conviction for his opinion. Consequently, when he saw her milling in the chaos of that afternoon, his heart lurched, and he screamed her name. She did not seem to hear him and as he pushed against the soldiers to cross the street, she disappeared into the dilapidated clip joint his mother had worked in till her death.

The two men at the door, designated to shake up tight-fisted clients, absconding clients, and the like, let him through because they were too surprised to stop him. A huge strobe light rotated from the iron sheet ceiling and dancing soldiers bumped against him under its intermittent glaring lights, swirling about to the music like they would to a war dance: in a frenzy of waving hands, kicking feet, and faces as dark and gleaming as Dafala's egg plants.

'The guards at the door swear that you've lost your mind, Father.' It was a woman who spoke to him, a woman like his mother, the kind of woman he always determined to forget.

'I'm looking for someone … a little girl. Her name is Salima.'

She put her arms around his neck—little stick arms that came from a little stick body. He could break it, he felt, by merely resting his hands on its sides. It spoke of paucity: conceived and bred as such into the natural state of her being.

'A desert man always thinks of the going out before he enters,' she said.

She talked like Dafala and her long hair smelt like his

mother's: of ancient Cushitic perfume encrypted into his pre-oedipal senses. 'I have to find her,' he said.

'You would need money.'

The only thing in his pocket was the bishop's letter. 'I have none,' he said.

'A trick then,' she suggested, 'something to fool a drunken soldier's eyes for a little while.'

'And you?' he asked, reaching for the bishop's letter. 'Doesn't a desert woman also think of the going out before she enters?'

'Me? I am like a Doum palm, Father. My head is always in the fire, but my feet run in the water.'

He opened the bishop's letter, removed its contents, and handed her the empty envelope. She let go of his neck and smiled —a little broken half smile that would always remain with him.

'Go back,' she said. 'I shall send her to you.'

In the vicarage living room, after lunch, and after the bishop's afternoon siesta, they sang him the poet Sedulius's 5th-century Easter poem: Hail, festival day, venerable throughout all ages, in which God vanquished hell and took possession of the Heavens/ Behold, the beauty of the reborn world bears witness to the fact that all the gifts of the Lord have returned with Him/ He who was crucified is God, and behold, He reigns over all things; let all creation lift its prayers unto the Creator/ O Christ, Saviour of all things, good Creator and Redeemer, only begotten of God the Father.

The bishop was in full regalia: his pink cap on the middle of his head, the bishop's ring on his hand. He smiled at the tiny set of dust prints across the red floor, which Fr Ahmed had polished to a gleam. The prints ended at Salima's bare feet. Tears welled in his eyes whenever she chorused *salve festa dies* … Dafala cried. Fr Ahmed, Fr Seif, and Fr Dugo cried. They all cried because they had never seen the bishop so moved.

But Fr Yasin did not really cry until sunset when he was lighting the sacred fire from which the paschal candle would be lit. When he knelt onto the dry sand, arranged the dry pieces of wood together, and lit them up, tears brimmed in his eyes. He wept then for the bishop, whom he loved. He wept for Dafala's pain. He wept for the woman with a little broken half smile who reminded him of his mother. He wept until a hard rubber boot bit into the back of his neck and yoked his head still. With bleary eyes he saw a familiar envelope fall before his face and into the fire. At that moment he remembered what the woman with a little broken half smile had said to him—that she was like a Doum palm with her head in the fire but her feet running in water.

A rifle barrel dug into his spine and the pressure at the back of his neck increased, forcing his face closer to the fire. The hair on his face singed all at once and the flames danced and leapt higher as they consumed the crumpled envelope. The hot ash beneath exploded. Something more than mortal man seemed to be holding him down. He faced, then, a fear that is only known to a nomad as he comes to the realisation that he is too deep out in the desert to make it across or to turn back.

Then the boot on his neck lifted unexpectedly and with it the rifle barrel. As Fr Yasin reeled away from the fire, smoke and heat in his lungs, he saw the bishop on the other side. He was standing very still, the desert sunset reflected so deep in his eyes that it seemed to be flaring from within him. In his hands was the towering white paschal candle. Engraved on it, in golden letters, was the alpha at the top and the omega at the bottom. In between the letters were five red grains of glowing incense, one for each holy wound. When the volley of bullets exploded over Fr Yasin's head, the paschal candle suddenly glowed with hundreds more; they sparkled red like rubies. The paschal candle remained standing even as the bishop let go and Fr Yasin blindly reached for his punctured body. It stood, stoic, the candle, at that eerie

21

moment when the dark figure was scaling the vicarage walls and the church bells were pealing to the rhythm of abrupt thunder rumbling from afar.

OUR LADY OF LOURDES 16TH ANNUAL KNIGHTS OF COLUMBUS SPAGHETTI DINNER

'So,' she said, 'you're one of them.'

Sylvia Faraja watched her friend Matt Kress lean back into his chair trying not to look annoyed, but his mouth settled into a thin line and his grey eyes lost their gallantry.

The woman's tone of voice had galled him, Sylvia could see. This old woman with long white hair stylishly wrapped on her narrow head had galled Matt: Matt, the impassive man. Sylvia tried to remember her name or how this conversation, argument really, had started but could not. It was awful. Here they were, at Our Lady of Lourdes church in Lewiston, Idaho, in support of the Knights of Columbus annual spaghetti dinner, because Matt was part of the Catholic brotherhood, only to have an old woman lock horns with him.

'Yes,' he replied. 'I work with the Forest Service and burning is good for forests. Besides, the worst ones only occur because previous fires have been suppressed time and again. This is the mistake we're making in America.'

Secondary growth—that was the term that had started this whole thing. Matt and his forestry terms, which were such an innate part of his work at the research station, and the old woman endowed with an ear for them. She had been talking about a fire on her property many years ago, the wind blowing a little prescribed burning totally out of control and the Forest Service not very interested in putting it out, or miserably failing to; Sylvia could not remember which. Whatever the case, in the midst of that innocuous visiting Matt had mentioned secondary growth and maybe accumulation of too much fuel so that he had suddenly looked very knowledgeable on the topic as he sat there, across the table, in his checked work-shirt and rimless glasses. It was then that the old woman in a purple sweater had blurted out the accusation, saying he was 'one of them.'

'The Forest Service would rather have trees burn than sell them to loggers like us. Can you believe that, sweetheart?' she asked Sylvia.

Sylvia looked into her lined face and did not know whether to appear sympathetic, especially with Matt looking increasingly unsympathetic. Despite the age on the old woman's face Sylvia could still discern the angular lines of its youthful days, the sharp nose of obstinacy that was hardly wrinkled at all, and her small blue eyes behind glasses very much like Matt's own. She wore an elaborate brooch on her purple sweater. There were brooches on the sweaters of the other old women at the table, too, Sylvia noticed, but the old woman in the purple sweater had a golden bird brooch edged with rhinestones, and it was by far the finest of them all. It shone on her breast like a stubborn monument of happier and more prosperous logging days.

Everything and everybody in the church hall had telltale signs of happier and more prosperous days. Sylvia had sensed that as she and Matt had made their ten-dollar donation at the counter, had their plates laden with spaghetti and meatballs, and eventually found themselves at the end of this table in close proximity to the old woman in the purple sweater who was now looking into Sylvia's eyes in search of an answer to her question. Sylvia, however, could only summon a vague smile.

'Pass the salt,' the old woman said at last, turning from Sylvia to Matt.

Matt passed the salt. 'It's not as easy as you think,' he said, 'selling the trees. We have to take into consideration what environmentalists are talking about.'

'Environmentalists don't know what they're talking about,' she snapped. 'All they do is sit in trees and wave placards.'

'That's the exact kind of attitude that has things all tied up in the federal courts,' Matt replied. 'Loggers say environmentalists don't know what they're talking about. Environmentalists say loggers don't know what they're talking about. Nobody is willing to listen to the other and so the Forest Service is dragged into the whole thing.'

'Coffee?' asked one of the knights.

Matt extended his hot cup, and the knight filled it up. He sipped his coffee slowly, much in the same way that he had when Sylvia had first met him a year ago. Sylvia was an exchange student from the Gambia studying anthropology. People and their history interested her. This old woman interested her. 'Is your husband a knight too?' she asked.

'No,' the old woman replied. 'We're Episcopalians.'

Sylvia nodded.

'Being an Episcopalian,' the old woman continued, looking at Matt who seemed surprised, 'isn't as bad as worshipping trees. There are some people who worship trees nowadays. Closer to a tree than any Indian has ever been.'

Sylvia saw that Matt was letting it all slide but not without effort. Grimness settled into the shadows of his handsome face and its chiselled edges tightened. An old knight in shirtsleeves appeared, red apron over blue jeans, mangy hair, teeth all but gone, and with gnarled hands proffered a basket of warm bread. *In Service to One, In Service to All*, the white emblem on his red apron read.

'Breaking bread together under Douglas firs!' the old woman in the purple sweater said, her thin pink lips curled.

It seemed to Sylvia that the old woman was about to spit in her anger, but she only turned to one side of her chair and rummaged through her purse for a piece of tissue into which she coughed severely. Her cough was rough and snotty and it made her chest heave. She returned the tissue into her purse, which looked like it might have once been white.

'The Forest Service can't offer loggers as much stumpage as they demand,' Matt said. 'There're just not enough trees.' He drank more of his coffee even though he did not seem to like it and poked halfheartedly at a meatball. His face had turned red and his eyes could not seem to meet Sylvia's. The entire table was silent, Sylvia suddenly realised, as if they had been listening to the conversation between Matt and the old woman in the purple sweater above the din of their own.

Sylvia turned to them and was met with the silent, coarsened looks of old loggers and old loggers' wives. She spotted odd faces marked by jumping saws and rough hands with missing fingers. She imagined these loggers' hands on their women's bodies and suddenly Matt's smooth hands embarrassed her. They were strong hands, naturally enough. They shovelled snow off his drive, weight-lifted, and even went skiing often. But they were smooth, and everybody at the table was looking at them as he played around with a meatball.

It was then Sylvia had to get up and go to the bathroom even though her bladder was empty and unwilling. She was scrubbing her hands under the faucet when she looked up into the mirror. Looking deep into her own eyes, she could envision Matt's own grey eyes. She could imagine those grey eyes narrowing each year as he presented research data to the Forest Service, advocating for fewer trees to be logged, and the Forest Service, consequently, offering fewer trees for sale. The loggers, with not enough to live on, would look for work farther and farther away from home; their women would pawn their brooches, and no new purses would be bought for years.

Loggers had to do with less and less in the Gambia, too. Her elder brother, for instance, had closed down his sawmill in Georgetown and moved back home to Bathurst on St Mary's Island. He was now a trader like her father and her three other brothers were; a trader like most of her Wolof ancestors had been.

26

He rarely went up the river to Georgetown now; it was a place he wished to remember not, Sylvia had concluded.

Sylvia, herself, loved going up the Gambia River. Sometimes she would ride the ferry past Georgetown all the way to the last stop in Basse Santa Su. On each side of the river were mangrove swamps with their aerial roots peeking above the surface of the water and pygmy hippos lingering under the shadows. Beyond the mangrove swamps were forests of cedar and mahogany. It, however, seemed to Sylvia that with each passing year the shadows beyond the swamps had become lighter and lighter, and grass-covered river flats appeared where there had been none before. The golden-winged sunbird, which glittered under the sun like the brooch on the old woman in the purple sweater, no longer flew over the ferry that often either. There were times Sylvia would ride the ferry and not see the sunbird's flaring orange and yellow colours at all.

Now, as Sylvia dried her hands slowly in the bathroom at Our Lady of Lourdes, she wondered how Matt was doing in the face of all those old buckers, fallers, choker setters, their old wives, and the old woman in the purple sweater. She should have been out there supporting him, she knew, if only in honour of her memories of the golden-winged sunbird in Gambia. So she drew her lean Wolof figure to its full height, smoothed her black pant suit, and left the bathroom determined to set her face in favour of Matt even though she was certain that he could parry and remain on his horse long enough.

'What do you mean that is a peripheral opinion?' an old logger was asking Matt when she got back.

'Exactly that,' Matt replied. 'Canadian multinationals and their low-wage loggers, or timber from the Amazon isn't the reason our timber industry is bleeding right now. It's our own loggers. They have been logging way beyond sustainable estimates for years. The result is that the Chief of the Forest Service can only approve so much standing timber for sale each year.'

'The problem,' one old man said, 'is that there is no patriotism in American industry nowadays. We built this land, goddamn it! We built the roads and the towns. What have environmentalists done for America?'

'What we need is a man to stand up to the Chief of the Forest Service and Washington,' someone else said. 'A politician we can trust.'

'Pie in the sky!' the old woman in the purple sweater cried. 'The last time we sent someone to the Forest Service they called him a cedar thief.'

Matt's eyes met Sylvia's. A slough of despondency seemed to wash through them as he left the table for their dessert.

The old woman in the purple sweater started coughing again. Hard. She coughed like she had bronchitis, the kind brought on and acerbated by that white ominous plume of sulphur dioxide slowly dissipating over the town from the mill. Her small bird-like chest puffed and heaved till it looked like it would rip wide open right there and then. When, in due time, she was finally able to stop, tears and pain stained her eyes.

'Tell me about the Gambia,' she said to Sylvia.

When Hanno the Carthaginian had passed by the Gambia in 480 BC he had gazed at the majesty of the Gambia River flowing into the Atlantic and called it the gateway to Africa. Sunbirds had filled the sky then, Sylvia believed. It was that old country of frontier forest and a crystal clear river that Sylvia liked thinking of; country such as this old woman in a purple sweater had once been a part of. Was it possible for one to really forget it? 'The Gambia,' Sylvia said, 'is small, but the Gambia River runs through it, seven hundred miles of it. Sometimes, when I close my eyes, I can hear the rushing water and the song of the golden-winged sunbird.'

28

WHEAT FIELDS

I am a criminal lawyer. During my long career I have watched many men struggle to fit this mould, meandering through years of books and tortured morals so that they settle in at last like a man's foot in a lady's shoe. Not I, Dick Addison. I came to criminal law without major trepidation over books or morals, but with the one and most primary qualification: an irrepressible yearning to argue a man from the chains that might shackle him forever. Whether such a man deserved it or not was a matter that I preferred leaving to the judge's discretion until *The People vs. Alvah Imatu* in 1964.

The whole business with Alvah was years ago, but it refuses to leave my mind even though tomorrow is my seventieth birthday, and my son Colin and his family are here on the farm for the weekend. His wife, Pauline, is in the kitchen making the cake herself even though Miriam, my long-time housekeeper, which is really not an appropriate term for her, can make one perfectly well. As a result of that slight, Miriam has brewed my coffee so impossibly strong this morning that it stings all the way to my gut. It would seem senseless to complain about one morning of bad coffee out of the thousands of good coffee mornings I've had and so I do not. I tell myself it could be a delight; somewhat like the Turkish coffee I once took in the Somali bazaars of Nairobi's Eastleigh. Yes, I resolve, Turkish coffee; a particularly potent cup that might even have brought a smile to the rich Somali merchant I had gone to meet in the bazaars that day. Men for coffee, women for talk, the Somali say. But, eventually, the Somali merchant had talked, swearing, in the name of the Holy Koran, that he was not the man responsible for a bloody robbery in downtown Nairobi. Some envious business competitor had simply slandered his name at the police station. Or maybe some corrupt police officers themselves were seriously after him this time around—they were like an old wound that never went away. He had vowed all this and then pushed ten thousand pounds my way. Right, ten thousand pounds with none other than Her Majesty's very face on them because that is how money is kept in the bazaar—in ever-appreciating pounds.

The merchant was astounded by the fact that I had been in the country for so long. While most of the white settlers were fleeing Kenya's bloody wave of independence and selling their farms for mere pittance or simply deserting them, my father, my mother—in her grave deep in the soil—and I had stayed right on. Those who did not flee were eventually bought out and on they went to Southern Rhodesia or South Africa, to New Zealand or Australia, even back to England. But we had stayed.

I am thinking of this as I sip Miriam's Turkish coffee without so much as a flinch. It is hard to believe that so many years have passed. I wish Colin would breakfast with me; however, he is sleeping in. He never sleeps as well in Nairobi as he sleeps here. He has never told me so; I simply know it from my own experience, because he is like me and even though we can lie just about everything else we cannot lie about sleep or the farm. Nairobi, three hours away from here in a good car, is not the place to catch some good sleep. Not for me or Colin anyway.

It is peaceful here on the farm, where I was born on a rainy April morning in 1931. The house sits up on this hill and the wheat fields roll up and down smaller hills and across the tiny hollow intervals in-between. I am not the desperate and mortgaged English settler farmer my own father was, but I have kept the wheat growing nonetheless. Colin has often accused me of growing wheat for the heck of it.

I suppose it might sometimes look to him that it *is* for the heck of it; however, that is the way the fields have always been since I can remember them. Without the wheat I would feel naked

30

and exposed up here on the hill just as he, Colin, would feel in a courtroom without his pinstripe suits from Nairobi's Henry's and Little Red. Can you imagine a lawyer trying to make a serious statement without his clothes on? That is how I feel without the wheat. I hate the sight of hired combine harvesters, from nearby Nanyuki Town, rolling over the hills, shoring away at the golden fields whose harvest I can no longer procrastinate about because the skies are growing muggier with each passing day and the wind is blowing with the firm consistency that brings the rains. But I hate the plough tractors even more as they bury wheat stubble and sow the seed, ever engulfed in billows of dust, their drivers in a brutal hurry to beat pregnant rain clouds gathering over the far August horizon. That is how my wheat is always sown—just in the nick of time, sometimes with the thunder rumbling and the rain pounding and a few brave, scavenging larks in the wake of it all. These hired men and their machines leave everything a deep grey colour so that the farmhouse, up here on the hill, looks like one of those snowcapped peaks of Mount Kenya, which I see every morning from the terrace.

Colin had once vowed that he would put an end to this wheat fetish of mine. We were walking the fields together that day, and he had said that, upon my death, he would plough it all out and let the fields run wild with tussock grass. Then he would get a government permit to keep and breed wildlife on the farm: wildebeest, hirola antelopes, and giraffes. Perhaps he would even acquire one of those precious black rhinos. He would do like some farms were doing in Lewa Downs and make loads of money from wildlife ranch tourism or else he would lease out the entire land to one of those emerging corporations that were growing green beans, cut flowers and strawberries for export in massive greenhouses. I am not sure if he was serious or not that day. His eyes were the same spangled and hooded yellow as mine—revealing nothing.

31

As I sit drinking my morning coffee, I begin to wonder what would happen if I stood up right now and walked in on Colin sleeping, roused him awake, and asked him if he really meant what he had said to me that day. I am so gripped by this thought that I soon find I have actually stood up from my wicker chair on the terrace and walked to the wide camphor doors of the bedroom Colin has occupied since he was a child. I can hear his daughter's voice inside. Sigrid is her name, my granddaughter. She is seven years old. The doors are slightly ajar, and I can see her through the open crack in her pink evening shoes and pink cotton pyjamas, and with the little auburn curls of her hair in overnight disarray. Colin's head is slumped deep in the pillow, Pauline's empty space beside him a crumpled array of white sheets, but his back is to that and his yellow eyes are on Sigrid. She is singing and acting out an old rhyme Colin himself sang while in nursery school: the one about head and shoulders, knees and toes, knees and toes, knees and toes.

The rhyme stops me cold in my tracks. It is an uncanny reminder of *The People vs. Alvah Imatu* in 1964. Thirty-seven years ago the case's prosecuting attorney informed the judge that the police had retrieved Alvah Imatu's wife from an abandoned pit latrine on the farm piece by piece: head, shoulders, knees, and toes. The memory sickens me, and I suddenly find that I cannot enter Colin's old room. I turn back and softly walk down the corridor, past the terrace, and out into the fields where the wheat is so high and ripe that it reaches my waist. Standing there, I recall that the prosecuting attorney broke into tears as he presented photographic evidence to the judge. The prosecutor, a hard man in every way, had wept.

Not once, through the entire trial, had I seen Alvah weep. I remember the first time that I really talked to Alvah, here on the terrace of the farmhouse. He had a black suit on and matching shoes so new that they must have been pinching him. His bodyguard and driver, both in colonial khaki police uniform and with guns on their hips, stood beside the blue government Land Rover, which was still marked with England's imperial insignia even though it had been six months since Kenya's independence.

The only land we had on that day, June of 1964, was this hill where the farmhouse stands. All the rest, two hundred hectares of it, was gone, repossessed by the bank and sold to the new government. Unfortunately, it had not been granted to poverty-stricken squatters, who were slowly leaving colonial era detention camps, but to politically connected men like Alvah.

Hugh Frederick's farm, neighbouring ours to the east, was under Alvah's proprietorship, too. His family in England had stopped subsidising what they now regarded a risky venture in post-colonial Kenya and told him to ship out with everyone else. The day that Hugh Frederick agreed to this and let the British government buy him out under the agreed upon land reform procedures, he had locked himself in his bedroom and put a bullet through his head instead of shipping out. His wife and two daughters had buried him, packed a single suitcase each, and asked me to drive them to the Nairobi Embakasi Airport.

I was always driving to the airport or to the railway station those days, helping people leave. Everyone was leaving, including my ex-wife, Colin's mother, who ran off with a rich Italian man she met while holidaying at Malindi. Colin's mother never really had much heart for the wheat fields of Nanyuki to begin with. She was a lot like Pauline, Colin's wife, is right now: with no genuine feeling for the place.

My father did not shoot himself in the head like Hugh Frederick when he lost his farm; instead, he sat on his rocking chair in the living room facing the wall and refused to leave the house. Looking back, I suppose this was the only reason the bank did not repossess the house and the hill it stood upon. Nobody wanted another suicidal farmer on their conscience—he could

33

keep the damned house on the damned hill, the bank must have decided as they hived them off from the rest of the farm. I could not bear to see him that way and so I mostly kept to Nairobi, where I concentrated on establishing my practice until the day Alvah Imatu walked into my law firm chambers because he had cut up his wife—head, shoulders, knees, and toes. That he came to *me* of all people was quite a shock. I had refused to take his case and so he had come to see me here, a second time, at the farmhouse. We sat on the terrace facing Mt Kenya and what were now his wheat fields. There was something about a man cutting up one's wife and ditching her in a pit latrine piece by piece that totally crippled my ability to be his advocate, criminal lawyer though I am. I detested him, but then there was the farm to consider and he knew that I would inevitably soften my stand if he dangled the right carrot. For my services, he was going to hand it back. Upfront, he offered me a newly made out title deed, already with my name on it, knowing that he would not be refused this time around.

The wheat fields, sown by Alvah, had been afflicted with the worst case of stem rust I had ever seen that year. The kernels were shrivelled and pustules of dusty spores, so deep orange that they were red, dotted the wheat like lesions on a leper. The fungi had blossomed in a malignity of red spores that spread over everything: the leaf sheathes, the stems, and the shrivelled kernel were all covered with it. This fungi attack was at the height of an unrelenting repeater stage, the stems had weakened and lodged, and swarms of insects nestled in the besieged fields, attracted by the tiny drops of honey dew dripping from the pustules. The wind blew like the khamsin, hot and in gusts. The gusts would intermittently startle the insects out of the wheat into a restless buzz, and the wheat itself would flow like a sea of blood over the hills, stiff and lodged stems snapping.

There was a terrible smell of widespread rot in the air

34

as Alvah and I sat there and talked. When he left in his blue government Land Rover, I walked into the house and told my father that we had gotten our farm back. I told him that it had been out with the old wife and in with the new one for Alvah Imatu, hence the remains that the police had found in the pit latrine on his farm. My father had not said a thing to all that, but when I departed for Nairobi he had set the fields on fire as if to cleanse them and then died in his sleep a week later.

The wheat fields were cloaked in mounds of black ash during his funeral. I can still see them in my mind as I saw them that night from the terrace of the farmhouse, rolling on into infinite darkness and with the acrid smell of burnt wheat still hanging in the air. I could stay out here forever and reminisce about that moment, but I have yet to take a bath and don something suitable for my birthday. It has to be something that will make me genuinely appreciate the pictures Pauline is bound to make Colin take. What this results in, however, is Miriam standing in my bedroom closet trying to convince me not to wear my old blue kilt because Pauline will probably find me comical.

'Forget Pauline,' I say, 'Colin, too. Damn them. Did I tell you that Colin might get rid of the wheat fields one day?'

Miriam laughs at this outburst and stops rummaging through the rest of the closet. She's thirty-seven and I am seventy and I want to kiss her madly. 'Come here,' I tell her and tap the space on the bed beside me. I catch laughter lingering on her lips and in the deep brown of her wide set eyes as she sits next to me. I lean toward her angular chin and kiss at one side of her throat and then the other, tracing the soft concentric lines there with my tongue. I have long wanted to marry her, but she will not let me. She gives no particular reason for her refusal, and so I have persistently argued with her over the matter, sometimes with the relentless skill of the lawyer in me, sometimes with the total tactlessness of a desperate lover.

I begin to wonder if Colin will ever get a chance in life to behave this absurdly—as only a lawyer totally in love would, that is—when I finally return to the terrace and find him there with a tall glass of orange juice. He is squinting against the sun in his face. I watch him watch me in my kilt. He says nothing. I suppose that he knows he does not look any prettier in his rumpled silk gown and that unruly head of dark brown hair, which he got from his mother.

'I've been looking at the Alvah case file,' he says, startling me. 'And that wife of his whom he cut up into pieces … Riano Sirankasio, that was her name.'

I notice the file now. It is yellow with age and turned up at the edges: *The People vs. Alvah Imatu*, it reads. By its colour and condition, I can tell it is not from our meticulously kept archives. It is the prosecutor's case file, I suddenly realise. How the hell did Colin get hold of that? I do not want to think of Riano Sirankasio—of her head, shoulders, knees, and toes—right now. I avert my eyes to the wheat fields.

'You have no idea what she looked like alive, do you?' Colin asks.

'No,' I say, 'it was easier not to.'

'I suppose you have no idea of what happened to those pieces of her body either,' he continues.

Those, I had heard of. The court had relinquished them to Riano Sirankasio's mother, who lived in the outskirts of Nanyuki Town in a Dorobo village. The old woman had arranged the bones on a bed that her daughter had slept on as a girl and covered the broken skeleton with lambskin. The prosecutor had tossed this bit of news at me outside the courthouse a few days after the ruling. He told me that the old woman sat in the darkness of her little mud hut and poured libations of honey wine to all her ancestral spirits, who were present at the birthing of the world. According to ancient Dorobo tribal lore, the prosecutor said, when God came on Earth to create man, he found the Dorobo and it is they who helped him get the job done. The old woman, the prosecutor told me with a most intent look in his eyes, was waiting for the day when her daughter would be avenged before she could die and rest in peace. I, of course, did not find this tale credulous at the time; however, my life did go completely awry three months after winning Alvah's case. I suddenly suffered a massive heart attack in my office one afternoon and was subsequently forced to let go of half of my former clients to ease my work load. You are so young, so in shape, my doctor had said in disbelief. I told him that I was stressed due to my father's passing and he believed that even though I knew that was not it. The old woman mourning in the darkness of her mud hut together with her ancestral spirits, who preceded all, had come to live within me.

Ironically, nothing bad seemed to have happened to Alvah. When I bumped into him at the Norfolk Hotel a couple of years later, he seemed as happy and as prosperous as ever. He had retired from politics by then, but was still wearing his signature pinstripe suits and matching new shoes. He had proudly introduced his only child, a daughter, Effie, who had been born to him rather late in life, and the new wife, who really could no longer be called new. Alvah was in an expansive mood that day: he had just purchased one of the biggest dairy farms in the country.

It was incredible, I had thought, that his life after the trial was such smooth sailing. Nothing special about an old woman mourning in her little mud hut, he had said when I enquired after the matter, nothing special at all. What did the old witch expect? Alvah had asked me. That her adulterous daughter will come back to life? Be reborn? He had thrown these questions at me with a terrible voice and spittle coming from his mouth. The enquiry had cost Alvah his expansive mood as he soundly dismissed the old woman. It was the last time I spoke or ever saw him again.

I look at Colin now and it occurs to me that I should tell him of the old woman sitting in the darkness of her desolate hut in the realm of wild spirits. This woman is so old that she should surely be dead by now. She is one-hundred-and-twenty years old and still pours libations of honey wine, still seeks vengeance for the first and last born of her womb—Riano Sirankasio. Riano was a love-child, the prosecutor had said. The old woman will *never* forget her. Riano was born when unkind villagers were whispering that her mother's womb was old and dried up. The old woman will *never* forget her. I know this today, and it is on the very tip of my tongue to tell Colin, but I am not sure how to begin.

'A lawyer,' I say, as a way of venturing into the subject, 'is very much like that man of whom Kingsley Amis wrote when he said that "his mouth had been used as a latrine by some small creature of the night, and then as its mausoleum".'

Colin, however, does not seem to be listening to me. 'Effie, Alvah Imatu's daughter, is dead,' he says, leaning back into his chair and running his well-manicured courtroom fingers through his hair. 'She was killed in her apartment in Nairobi. Slaughtered and carved up like some animal ... head, shoulders, knees, and toes. They say her ex-boyfriend did it, an ugly crime of passion. The young bugger claims that he has no idea what came over him.'

I am in shock. The wind sweeps over the wheat fields. They ripple back and forth and gleam in the sun. 'And I suppose that this young bugger has come to you,' I say, sensing where he is headed.

'Yes,' Colin says. 'I'm going to defend him.'

'You are walking into a snake pit,' I say. 'You know how Alvah will fight you.'

Colin downs his orange juice. 'Yes,' he says, 'I know how Alvah will fight me.'

It is then that Pauline comes onto the terrace with something that I recognise as my birthday cake. It is white and humongous

38

and they will have to leave for Nairobi with most of it. There are seven tiny red candles on it, each representing ten years.

'Oh, you look adorable, Addison,' she says to me. Pauline is the only person I know who consistently calls me by my last name.

Colin smiles as he reads my face. 'Where's everyone else?' he asks.

'Oh, yes, Sigrid … and Miriam, of course. I shall find them.'

I watch her leave in her black heels. When she is out of earshot, I turn to Colin. 'You don't have to take the case,' I say. 'We're done with Alvah. We're done with every sordid bit of that business.'

'Are we now?' he asks.

'Meaning what?' I ask, puzzled. I do not want to pass on the haunting legacy of the old woman mourning in her dark hut on to Colin. She is like a lead cross within me, but I am determined to take her with me to my grave. My death will be her death.

He reaches for the file, removes an old photograph, and slides it to the middle of the table.

It is true that I had never looked at Riano Sirankasio's photo—I never had the stomach for it after listening to the prosecutor. I had only thought of her in terms of hard and cold courtroom facts. Now I lean forward and pick the photo. I am looking, I find, at an old black-and-white photo of a woman who looks like my Miriam. Logically, of course, it *cannot* be Miriam. But staring at the photo I see the same face, I see the same eyes, which I love, and I see the same smile that makes my heart glow.

I first met Miriam twenty some years after Riano Sirankasio's murder. I had advertised for a housekeeper after our long-time housekeeper, who had managed the house for years since my father's days, finally retired. Miriam arrived with the long rains just after I had decided to sow the wheat regardless of the possibility of stem rust resurgence, which was still plaguing the fields. I was going to let it grow and reek if need be. I was seated on the terrace and had watched her climb up the hill to the farmhouse in her white dress. The sun, oddly breaking through that day, had been shining all morning and the mud on the road up the hill to the farmhouse had dried up in patches, leaving puddles of still, muddied water. It was easy to walk without getting a lot of mud on your shoes if you knew how to. She arrived on the terrace with relatively clean shoes and everything about her as warm as the sun itself.

At close range she looked even younger than twenty. I asked about previous employers. She replied that there were none. So I began talking housekeeping to test her knowledge and then quit because she had sat there answering every question I posed with growing boredom. I eventually lost her attention to the budding wheat fields, which I had fallowed intermittently since my father's death in an effort to fight the stem rust. She was admiring them; I was instantly convinced of this for some inexplicable reason. Impulsively, I had gotten to my feet, retrieved my best bottle of red wine, and brought two glasses with me out on the terrace. She watched me open the bottle and then leaned forward, ever so gently across the table, and took it away from me. Too surprised to resist, I let her have it. She walked off the terrace with it, slowly striding across the lawn to the edge of the wheat fields, a little beyond where my father and my mother lay deep in the earth, and gently poured the entire bottle of wine into the earth like an ancient Roman wheat farmer's wife pouring wine libations to appease Robigus, the goddess of Mildew. Then she came back to the terrace, set the empty bottle between us, and there we sat, in a deep, peaceful silence.

I am thinking about this now and how the wheat continued to grow green and healthy from the day Miriam arrived, like a messenger from an appeased god, when Pauline reappears.

'They must have taken a walk,' she says, throwing up her hands. The effort of making the cake and the heat in the

40

kitchen has her face almost as red as berries. 'Addison—' she begins to say.

'Yes,' I mutter, standing up on very weak knees. 'I'll go get them. They must be out there somewhere … in the fields.'

I hand the photo back to Colin like it is nothing much. He takes it back with the same nonchalance and puts it back in the file. I wonder how long it has been since he came across it. He has been here on the farm for a day and a half already, and you'd think it is the kind of thing he would have spat out at the front door when I had let them all in. But, no, he hands it to me like a present for my seventieth birthday. It occurs to me that I have never seen Colin in this light before. There is a steely determination in his eyes, like that of an unswerving soldier. A path is made by walking, our old housekeeper used to tell me as a child. O God, I think, everything is so beyond me. Colin is taking a path into the wilderness, and there is nothing to do but to let him walk it.

I leave him and Pauline on the terrace and head into the wheat fields. *Miriam*, I suddenly want to shout. *Miriam!* What I know to be true about her, my mind simply refuses to believe. Isn't the old woman in the darkness of her mud hut laughing at me right now? Aren't the ancient Dorobo spirits mocking me? I continue my way deeper into the wheat fields. Let the old woman laugh. Let the ancient spirits mock me. Even the wheat fields seem to be in on it as some leaves are so dry and sharp that they cut at my legs where the socks end and the kilt begins. I force myself to walk slowly. Gently. I stretch my hands out before me like I used to when I was a boy, so that I can feel the sea of awns beneath the palms of my hands and smell the air, which is rich with the scent of ripening kernels. I find them at last on a small rocky patch where the wheat is thin and short like a balding spot on a man's head. Sigrid is making a plait out of the wheat and Miriam is basking next to her, eyes closed. It is Miriam I love

41

above all else. I lay down there between them, aware for the first time today of the toll of each one of my seventy years, and put my arms around them both.

LEAVING LAMU

The sun was beginning to set, and the high-walled streets of Lamu were filled with shadows. Our streets had always felt like some ancient architect's afterthought to me. They were so narrow that a car could not drive through. Someone had left a street tap running, and a streak of water meandered its way down the pavement. What bad luck, I thought to myself, should someone slip and fall on the eve of Maulidi when we celebrated the birth of the Prophet.

Women were calling to each other across the street, their unveiled heads peering out of the open lattice windows above me: one borrowing salt, another asking to have her ladle back, another in need of having her hair braided. Everything was abuzz. Then, quite unexpectedly, there was Fatima Bakari coming up my way. She seemed to fill the entire street.

I had seen her before, of course, but it was always from afar. She came back to Lamu, where she had been born, every Maulidi to take part in the taarabu music performance that accompanied the festivities. Whenever I had thought of Maulidi, even as a young girl, I had thought of Fatima Bakari in her bright-coloured *bui buis* and her massive body swaying to the rhythm of potter's drums, guitars, and accordions. Women in Lamu unconsciously hummed taarabu—that lively island mix of Swahili and Indian bhangra; they sang it at circumcision rites and at weddings. Nobody, however, I must confess, sang like Fatima Bakari did. She was renowned for her talent not only in Lamu, but on the mainland as well.

I flattened myself against the coral-rag wall to let her pass. She looked me in the eye, and I got the feeling that I should perhaps have turned back. Anyone else in Lamu would have turned back for they both revered and shunned her at once. But I could not turn back, I found. It was as though I was rooted to the very street; a hapless prisoner under her heavy black kohl eyes. She walked right past me, so that I was momentarily engulfed in her huge body and then freed from it. I was left churning in the mighty surf of her perfume and the memory of her as endlessly soft. It was a memory that would not leave me for days and days. That and her eyes, which seemed to have looked into my very soul and smiled as if saying: *so*, you want to be like me!

I found my elder sister, Naima, seated on a straw mat under the shade of the mangrove cloister facing the courtyard when I arrived home. She was weaving a basket from coconut raffia. Naima was soon to marry the son of the muezzin at Riyadha Mosque. I kissed her on the cheek. I felt sad these days at the thought of her imminent departure. It was a mutual sadness, I think, but she had accepted it the way one accepts one's fate while I, on my part, had failed to. It was a failure I hid by walking directly into the coolness of the house.

Our house was a series of long and narrow dark rooms, like the streets outside. There was a large water cistern for the toilet, and we kept fish in there to eat mosquitoes. This is the way things had been for ages. I was born in this house and had known no other until I had started working as a chambermaid at the Lamu Palace Hotel. My father's family had lived here for hundreds of years, one generation and then the next. My grandparents lived on the first floor with my youngest uncle and his new wife, Zowala, while my family lived on the second floor. The third floor, covered with a *makuti* roof, served as a large communal parlour. I could hear my two younger sisters playing up there under the coolness of the coconut leaves.

My mother and Zowala were in the kitchen cooking for Maulidi. I could smell dinner, rice with coconut milk, already boiling in the pot on the charcoal stove standing on the balcony. My mother was by the mangrove stand garnishing fish with cloves,

44

chili and *dhania*. Zowala was kneading dough for chapatti. She had worked at the Lamu Palace Hotel before her marriage to my uncle. It was she who had requested that I replace her when she had become too heavy with child. Jobs, like houses in Lamu, were passed on from one family member to the next.

'Guess who I have just met?' I told my mother and Zowala, unable to contain it any longer.

'Who?' they asked.

'Fatima Bakari,' I replied.

My mother frowned, stopped what she was doing, and poured me a cup of gingered coffee. 'Ah, Suelah,' she said. 'You should not be seen with the woman.'

'And yet she sings for the Prophet tomorrow and will be seen with everyone,' I said.

'*Subhan* Allah,' my mother said, raising her hands upwards to the heavens. If there was anyone she prayed for, it was me.

Zowala pushed a platter of dates my way with the tip of one of her flour-whitened fingers, but avoided my eyes. Her once slender and beautiful face had swelled and pimpled with the pregnancy so that she hardly looked her former self.

'Would you have your job back, Zowala, saying that I, for some reason, no longer needed it?'

'Ya Allah! The questions you ask, Suelah! Who will ever marry you?' my mother asked.

Zowala was now staring at the plasterwork, which she so scrubbed downstairs despite her big belly that my grandparents often complained she was going to ruin it.

'You should finish your coffee and get us some more cooking oil, Suelah, my daughter of questions,' my mother said.

It was freeing, I had discovered over the years, to run errands. The shop we bought our groceries from was by the waterfront, ten minutes from our house. There were old boats there, old boats anchored in old moorings. It was a sight I never tired of. How beautifully they danced on the darkening water! I entered the shop and requested the cooking oil. The shopkeeper sorted through cans of tomato paste, sugar and salt before getting to the oil. He moved about carefully, in the dimly lit interior, like a brooding hen turning over her eggs.

'The boats dance for the Prophet tonight,' I said.

'Ah … the boats,' he sighed deeply, wiping the tin of oil with a small towel. He always wiped things and always with the same old rag of a towel. 'I've been watching them all my life. They bring me fish and they bring me this and that. But who ever leaves in them, uh? Who?'

He handed me the oil. I looked back over my shoulder to Lamu's old waterfront and the boats resting there in the water like divine stars in the night sky. 'Fatima Bakari,' I said.

'Pardon me?'

'Fatima Bakari,' I repeated.

His face was caked with age, but I saw that his eyes burned as they recognised in me what only Fatima Bakari had. 'Aah … it is *you*, Suelah,' he would always say to me from that day onwards. He would move his paraffin lamp closer to my face then, as if by catching a clearer glimpse of it he could be able to tell exactly when I would be leaving Lamu.

Her face was averted beneath the reed hat but he could already tell that she did not like him any more than he liked her. They were standing under the narrow verandah of the forest station, and a knot of autocatalytic despair was tightening in his gut. His despair was mostly brought on by the rain, which had been falling non-stop for three days. There was dark mud everywhere, as on the shores of the Congo River, and he could smell it deep in his lungs.

The station's warden was huddled inside the dank stone building, a walking marionette in threadbare fatigues. 'Martin … Dr Martin Honge,' he now jabbered. 'You're the man from BIOTA Africa, aren't you?'

Be gracious, Martin, he told himself. Gracious. So he took a step back inside and said: 'Yes. If you should recall, sir, I had asked for someone—'

'Who has, preferably, worked with olive baboons before,' the forest warden said before he could finish, his glazed cataracts impatient. 'What is this? You think she has not?'

Bugger the warden, he thought, back on the verandah. The girl, woman—he really could not tell which—would have to do. He wondered where she had found the small yellow dress; it clung to her skeletal body like old crepe, in thin web-like patterns. She needed, he thought, a new yellow dress.

'I want us to begin by identifying a suitable baboon troop to observe,' he said.

'Suitable?' she asked.

'One with the most females,' he elaborated. 'I'm collecting data on mating behaviour.'

She stepped out into the rain, as if glad to escape the little confining verandah, and headed for a tapering path leading into a dense shrub of wet *Dracaena fragrans*. She walked with sure-footed steps, treading the running mud proudly. She held her head high, as fearless as a jungle queen, while her Gabon Viper fang earrings dangled from each side like twin charms.

He had worried that she might be afraid of the forest, but she obviously was not. He saw that now; it was evident in her walk, a trait he had learnt to recognise in guides. How easy it was to lose one's mind and body to this natural phenomenon when there was nothing to cast one's eyes upon all day but rows upon rows of tree trunks lined with a wet, moquette-like surface of lichen and moss. But for a good guide, nothing could help if you really got lost, not your over-anxious mind, not your soul, not civilisation—least of all civilisation, with its basic first-aid kit and emergency rations, anti-venom shots, tubes of the most potent antihistamines, a tranquiliser gun, a flare gun, a pistol … Well, a pistol perhaps would, but only if you were willing to pull the trigger as Kop Bachunn, his fellow researcher, had three weeks ago.

It was an angst which came upon you, Martin had concluded, experienced in its pure wholesome state in this wet bizarre foliage and scampering shadows. Some men, like Kop Bachunn, could not endure that. He had brought Kop, delirious with fever, from the middle of the forest, to a Red Cross hospital along the Congo River. When he had visited the following day he had found an empty bed, a bloody mess on the white sheets, and a hole in the mattress—you could have easily mistaken it all for a piece of avant-garde art. The doctor had brought him Kop's pistol on a silver hospital tray, a livid look on his black face, a note of contempt in his voice—like that of a man who had been thwarted in his task. He had refused to be bothered with a diagnosis of Kop's illness. 'What's the use?' he had asked. 'He is dead.'

They came upon the baboons suddenly: wet hairy bodies swaying from one tree to another. They barked and leaped and gathered their young closer to themselves. Even as a boy he had felt an instinctive response to that primate pandemonium at an animal orphanage in Nairobi, an understanding only possible in the first ages. Is it not possible, you think? Are we not capable of comprehending the inexplicable mysteries of our existence in the midst of nature? Aren't the not-yet-born, the living, the dead, all the days that are gone as well as all the days that are to come, carried in us somehow? It was what he had once believed, that he could fathom all life, somehow, that he loved it, and it had led him to this line of work.

However, he was not sure of any of that now because he would have welcomed rain like this once: it was what made the Congo the Congo—ever flourishing, ever its own physician right from the West African Coast to where it halted, here, at Kakamega, Kenya. Now the rain made him angry because his binoculars could not work as they should, and he had to move closer to the baboons than he would otherwise have at first contact. It usually took weeks for a troop to get used to his presence, and, even then, he was always careful to wear the same colour of clothes for easy recognition. They needed time and a consistent display of innocuous behaviour before they could feel at ease in one's company. Like people, very much like people. Once, at a conference, someone had asked: 'Why bother studying baboons? They are at it all the time. In short, base promiscuous savages.'

'Like us, you mean?' he had replied. 'Stuffing every skirt that comes our way? Why the hell should we bother with us?'

It took an idiot who had never seen the beastly magnificence of a baboon alpha male, one like he had met at the conference, to ask that. The baboon was seated on a slightly lower branch than the rest of his troop, his erect member in full view, aslant—like a cannon in waiting, and his dark unmoving eyes fixed on them, eyes as flaming as the fierce red patch of wet fur above his brow. He looked ominous and there was a grating roar rising in

49

his chest. He was much too close to the baboon, Martin realised. It was appalling, he knew, such carelessness. More so because it was a carelessness born out of experience—like an Indian circus boy who keeps sticking his head in a lion's mouth until he loses the horror of it, even begins to enjoy it, only to have the carnivore, quite naturally, bite it off one day as he is grinning and the crowds are cheering at his vain valour. Now, this baboon, with its glistening canines, was going to tear him apart. What was to be said of him? He reached for his pistol, but then remembered that he had left it in the station's guesthouse. He could not carry it around, could not bear feeling its weight on his hip, because it reminded him of Kop. It was then he heard the girl, whom he had almost forgotten; she made a terrible snake-like hiss as he tried to duck away from the baboon.

He plummeted blindly into the bushes and remained there for a while, shaken, unmoving, and listened to his heartbeat and the quiver of every organ within him. He remained there until she tried to help him up only to find that his legs could do no more than allow him to sit there in the mud. The baboon called out loudly from his new spot, where he had galloped, frightened away by the girl's snake-like hiss, and his call resonated through the forest in short, tonal pitches of descending volume. His females responded to him and even though they moved higher into the canopy, they all held their ground.

She sat opposite him, on a wet, rotting tree stump, her viper earrings a blur of swinging pendulums. They could have been small children in a sandbox then. Martin Honge seated there in the middle, humiliated, and with his knees hurting; she on the edge, her eyes suddenly kind, her expression accepting of his total haplessness at the moment; and he not ashamed to be in need of her commiseration.

* * *

50

He was living as Kop had lived in the Congo, the way they all lived when in pursuit of the Congo's secrets: in a researcher's infernal mess of baboon hormonal faecal samples in test tubes, bottles of formaldehyde, muddy field clothes, and muddy boots—everything damp. Kop had explored the Congo for years with his singing Congolese and the Fang woman, whom he had encountered alone in the forest as a mere girl. He was a magnificent seven-foot khaki-clad figure and a delight to watch. When Martin first met him at an awards ceremony in Berlin he was in his fifties, his hair beginning to grey at the temples, thinning a little at the top, but what power there had been in his shoulders, in his stride. You could see that he loved ceremonies; his deep-set eyes glittered, his black handsome face was animated, and he laughed heartily.

But even then, at a moment when the world most admired him, Martin had thought: there is something wanting in him, a deficiency that he can hide no more than a child with kwashiorkor can hide its hideous belly. Maybe it was the way he walked around his fellow scientists, his wife's hand in his, her coffee-brown face serenely beautiful and secure in the knowledge of his devotion. That he was devoted to his wife, Martin had no doubt. It is easy to see when a man is truly devoted: his eyes betray him. But it was exactly that which most disturbed Martin—what did the Congo, with its singing Congolese, Fang woman and all, mean to him then, other than mere scientific glory?

Finding him there in his tent, a month ago, stilled by sickness, Martin could not help but think that the Congo had ravished him the way he had ravished it; his skin clung to his colossal frame, sweaty, blistery, and as dark as a starless night. It was as if he was cringing away from his very self. 'My field notes … you *must* pack these, Martin. I am not as sick as I look—I mean to come back. I shall live, I tell you! I shall! You are here, aren't you?' he had said. Then, continuing in a sudden temper: 'Tell those morons outside to play some music for Christ's sake!'

They must have heard him shouting, like a psychosomatic conductor. The soft strain of a guitar had suddenly broken through the night followed by a rhythmic rattle of a tambourine and then the constant and soothing throb of a Congo drum, beating in tune with human pulse. That and their celestial voices had stilled him into a psychedelic trance. He had slumped back onto his sleeping bag and laughed. 'Ah, your Achilles heel, Martin. You suffer genuine *nostalgie ya mboka*. You're an improved specimen who will neither file his teeth nor shake his buttocks to the rhythm of *mboka*!'

'I prefer to think my *nostalgie* a saving grace,' Martin had said, and stepped out of the tent.

The Fang woman and the singing Congolese were seated around a big campfire. He had hoped to see the Fang woman's face, but he never did. Not once. It was hidden beneath an elongated heart-shaped mask, which was a blazing white under the flickering campfire lights. The mask had a long fine black nose in the middle and black eyebrows that seemed permanently arched in surprise at him. The Fang, he knew, traditionally wore their masks to communicate with their illustrious dead, or to persecute wrongdoers. Who did she want to persecute, he had wondered? Kop, for his lust and unrequited love? The way he screamed for his wife! It must have been like a lance going right through her heart listening to Kop go on like that. Or was it him, for his mission was to take Kop away from her? He did not believe in the punitive power of her mask; however, he did find that he could not bear her masked stare: it felt as if his very soul had been bared and she was looking at it.

'He needs to be in a hospital,' he had said to break the trance, to offer an explanation.

'Not even Schweitzer's great hospital in Lambaréné would save him,' she had replied.

'And you could?' he asked.

In response she had stood and walked away, anger in every step.

Lying in the station's guesthouse now, with the rain still pounding down, Martin felt remorseful. She had been right: the hospital had not saved Kop. The Congo River had only borne him to his death. Even the singing Congolese, in hindsight, had seemed certain of Kop's death. 'Where are you going after this? After him?' they had asked.

'To Kakamega,' he had said. Then looking ashore to where the Fang woman stood and back to the Congolese in their dugout canoe, he had asked: 'Are you not taking her as well?'

'She will not come,' they had replied. 'Not now.'

They were headed to Kinshasa. They were going to be famous, they said: like Los Nickelos, like Mose Fan Fan, like Bella Bella, Shama Shama … Martin had half lifted his hand to wave at the Fang woman when she had turned abruptly and started walking back into the forest, her white mask in one hand. She walked as if she had a new mission to attend to, while Kop lay there on the floor of the motorboat, and the river carried them downstream.

Martin could hear the rain coming from afar; it was like an endless company of horses driving a carriage over cobble: shored hoofs and steel wheels on cobble—steel on cobble, steel on cobble. Insistent and razor sharp as it fell on the iron sheet roof. A vicious wave of nausea gripped him and came rushing and twisting up his throat. He staggered out of his bed, one hand clamped over his mouth, and crashed, sightless, into the bathroom. He fell onto his knees next to the toilet bowl and held onto it as his stomach wrenched and convulsed in a severe pain that drained every iota of strength from his body. When he was finally able to open his eyes, he was greeted by the sight of thick saliva, a green undigested antibiotic capsule and blood floating inside the bowl. He flushed it down and pulled himself upright slowly.

He turned on the bathroom faucet and rinsed his mouth with cold water. When he looked at his eyes in the mirror he found that they were as red and sore as Kop's had been. A doctor, he thought, I need a doctor. Usually his first-aid kit sufficed for minor tropical ailments, but this, he felt, was something different. As he staggered out of the bathroom, his body awash with pain, he found her standing at the door leading to his room. She was in the same yellow dress she had been wearing three days ago. She was still wet and as thin as ever. The reed hat was clasped to her chest and he could see her hair now. It seemed shot through, agouti really, as he had seen on blue monkeys. In her other hand she had a white mask, which he instantly recognised.

'I should have guessed,' he said, more to himself than to her.

She placed her reed hat on his desk. Inside it was some kind of fruit and a little bark container, her asek-bieri in which she must have been carrying skull fragments of her illustrious ancestors. He had seen Fang relic containers before while working in the forests of Gabon; they were not to be touched by those who had never been 'introduced' to them. The white mask she propped against the wall, beside the reed hat. How she had come in possession of the Ngil mask was a wonder. It almost exclusively belonged to male members of her tribe's secret societies who wore them to communicate with their ancestors. She walked away from the desk slowly, throwing open all the wooden windows and letting in massive amounts of light and moist blustery air. Then she knelt by the fireplace and got a fierce fire running.

'What is your name?' he asked, sitting himself gingerly on the bed.

'Elgon,' she said.

'Well, what do you want, Elgon?'

'His things … where are his things?'

'Over in that trunk,' he said. 'Reminisce all you want. Knock yourself out.'

54

She got them out one by one, Kop's field notebooks, all his papers, his precious butterfly casings … all the Kop mementos that he had been mandated to read through and catalogue, and she flung them into the roaring fire. He lunged for her, in disbelief, but another wave of pain gripped him in the gut, and he collapsed onto the wooden floor. When the pain receded, he crawled, on all fours, back onto his bed and together they regarded the fire as it burned brighter and the glass casings exploded one by one.

'Why?' he asked.

'He wouldn't let me help him, but he wrote it down anyway … the ancient remedy for Fievre hemorragique de Congo.'

'Ebola?' he stammered.

'Yes, Ebola,' she said. 'Didn't your most trusted doctors tell you?'

He found that he could not answer. Hardly anyone survived the virus and a hospital could do nothing more than ease an inevitable death. 'Kop knew?'

'He didn't believe it.'

'He shot himself … in the hospital.'

'Maybe the bleeding began and he could deny it no longer,' she said.

Martin sat, still to his very soul.

'I can try to help you,' she said. 'Sometimes it works, sometimes it does not.'

He stared at her and then closed his eyes in despair, knowing that he had no choice but to do as she said. So, eventually, he ate what she offered from her reed hat and slept when she said that he should. He did not know for how long he slept, how many hours … how many days. He found himself in the bathroom when he woke up, naked in a tub of warm water. There were orchids floating on the water: *Eulophia streptopetala, Habenaria malacophylla, Disperis aphylla* … Their scent was deep within him. It had stopped raining, he noticed through the open

55

bathroom window, and the sun was shining.

He rose from the water and walked into the outer room, expecting to find her there. The door and all the windows were wide open and swinging on their hinges in the wind. Baboons were asleep on the wooden verandah. Dry leaves and butterflies floated in and out from the forest. The log fire had burnt itself out. He looked at his desk: her asek-bieri and mask were gone. He wanted so much, at that moment, to get her a new yellow dress.

SWEET SUGARCANE SECRETS

My mother and my aunt are on the front porch. They have been cutting cane all day long. I draw closer and closer to the floorboard crack beneath them, holding my breath hard, afraid of being discovered. When I look up the crack a shaft of soft light pours down my left eye, and I see them finally. They are both seated there, on sticks of furniture, facing that yellow-stemmed forest of cane, swatting flies. I can see their hands as they move in the hot air, all ridged and spurred, like old bark on old trees.

I like creeping up on them at times like this and listening to whatever it is that they are talking about. When they sit together like this at the end of the day, their faces stained with a mixture of sweat and sweet sugarcane juices, blindly staring past the blue forget-me-nots growing in the unkempt grass and then beyond to that cane, they seem to be exchanging deep secrets that only women know about.

I suddenly hear my own name albeit too late; it is a stark inflection in the placid undulation of their voices. My mother's summonses are always unforeseen.

'*Yawah*!' she exclaims in our native Dholuo, getting off her chair. She is using her favourite exclamation: one that denotes utmost wonder. *Yawah*! The floorboards creak under her feet. 'Are you down there again?' she asks.

I run out of my hiding place and into the safety of the long grass beyond the porch. I hear her running after me, I hear her long burgundy skirt billowing out like an umbrella, raging in the wind. I sink into the grass and hide my face against it, unmindful of bees or snakes. The grass smells sweet and sunny. I hear her still wandering about in it, asking questions I cannot answer without giving myself away.

'Have you fetched water?' she asks.

Yes, I have.

Then I hear our donkey cart is coming up the trail. It is Father! He is back. Can he see me from up there? He should have ferried all the cane my mother and aunt had been cutting to the factory, but—*yawah!*

If things were right, this is what he would ask my mother: How are you doing, my sweet sugarcane darling?

Very well, my sweet sugarcane darling, she would reply.

But—*yawah!*

I wade deeper into the grass, startling bees and butterflies into the air, and deeper still into the sweet sugarcane. It is all this sweetness in the cane which makes it bearable, I think: only that.

THE BOSKOPMAN

Karl Rommel could see that I was pleased with the land until we came across a man digging a pit latrine—the Boskopman, as Rommel called him. He was a thin man, this Boskopman: a sinewy apparition of weary muscles on long limbs. He was standing waist deep in the vast pit latrine, a dirt-soiled loincloth clinging to his hips, an old khaki hat on his head. The hat had a round, gold-coloured badge at the front and a wide rim that shaded his sunburned face. He stopped shovelling the brown earth when he saw us and let the shovel rest to one side of the pit.

'*Guten Morgen*,' he said.

There was something so startling about the absolute blueness of his mixed-race eyes that I did not return his greeting. He had chanced upon an unmarked grave, Rommel explained to me in his broken English. The Boskopman resumed shovelling dirt and bones out of the pit.

'He should board it up,' I told Rommel, watching loose soil crumble off the dirt walls with each shovel the Boskopman drove into the earth. The pit looked like it would collapse on him anytime.

Rommel muttered something in disgusted German.

The Boskopman straightened his sinewy back. '*Ja*,' he said. '*Ja ...ja.*'

He was still at it when we came back the following day, chest deep now, nothing done to secure the walls. He gave a wild laugh when I pointed to him and the pit and all those human bones. 'German Südwestafrika Protectorate,' he said. '*Vernichtungsbefehl ...Vernichtungsbefehl.*'

This, I later came to understand, was the native extermination order that had been issued by Kaiser Wilhelm II in 1904. The hat the Boskopman wore on his head was an imitation of the one that had been worn by German volunteer soldiers carrying out the order.

Luderitz was a strange place. There were human bones, I was told, from here to Skeleton Coast, where they shifted with the sandveld. Many of these bones, I learned, had come from natives who had died of severe lashings of the *sjambok*, hunger, disease or madness in a concentration camp on Shark Island. Their corpses, buried under shallow sand graves, had washed onto the shores of Luderitz.

Other bones came from men who had been worked to death and left out on the sand dunes during the construction of Luderitz Harbor and the railway line, which run to Aus and further on to Keetmanshoop.

The Boskopman, I finally realised, was begging for death and would never board up his pit latrines.

UP ON THE HILL

Irwin Labo had lost a lot of blood in the car crash and was in constant pain that was barely relieved by the drugs he took. He had been lying on the narrow steel hospital bed for two weeks now, and when he turned his bandaged head he could see sick men lying on similar beds on either side of the concrete aisle, some in twos for lack of space.

He had lost track of time but for day and night and the set regimen hours for drugs and injections when the nurses would come shovelling the men about, even those like Irwin who dropped an anchor and reckoned themselves unmovable for the additional pain of a hypodermic. It was day now; he could see that through the empty window opposite him on which there was nothing but thin gauze to keep the mosquitoes out. It was hot. He could hear the corrugated iron sheet roof crackling in the equatorial sun. Irwin spent most of his time staring at the underside of the iron sheets, tracing with his swollen eyes the brown rust spots that a ceiling might have hidden from view. All around him sick men lay on top of their worn linen sheets, sweating. Irwin began to wish for night when the stone ward would cool and the men would pull the linen and their threadbare blankets back onto themselves and sleep, drowsy from the dissipating heat, illness and medication.

An old man on the other side of the aisle stirred and rose from his bed with creaking noises. Irwin did not know what ailed him. The old man wore a worn blue-and-red checked shirt and nothing else. His black buttocks hung flat and wrinkled from behind, and his penis and testicles hung black and wrinkled from the front. Irwin watched the old man walk past his bed in slow, shaky steps, like a bird that had narrowly escaped drowning, and followed him with his eyes all the way down to the end of the long hospital ward where the toilets were located. He listened to the old man urinate long and hard into the urea-stained bowl. He emerged from the toilet without flushing, all genitalia, weak knees and a mob of uncombed white hair on his head.

The nurses had been in their little white cardboard tearoom adjacent to the ward entrance when the old man made his journey to the toilets. They had been talking and laughing and drinking tea with the doctor who had just finished his round. They were now standing in the aisle looking at him as he returned.

'That old man hasn't got any manners at all,' Irwin heard the young nurse say to the old nurse.

'I'll remind his wife to bring him underwear,' the old nurse said, and she wrote it down in the huge, square-ruled notebook she always carried under her armpit. Irwin did not think that the old man had anything in his possession that could remotely be said to be underwear and might have voiced his opinion if his mouth were not so sealed with pain and sickness. Thus, he could only content himself now with watching the two nurses. The old nurse was short and stocky. She might have once been slender and shapely, like the young nurse, but she was now stocky and very serious. She was holding a new IV cord on her free arm, and when the old man passed them she hit him with it across his shoulders as though she were a matron in an all-boys school.

The old man got into his bed as if nothing had happened. Perhaps he was in too much pain to feel the bite of the IV cord. If Irwin had been feeling better, more able to talk, he would have told the nurses to shove it because there was nothing a man could attain to get ahead in life here, manners least of all. After all, here he was, all manners and several law degrees and in no way better off than the other sick men in the ward at this particular moment.

Irwin had earned his first law degree from the University of Nairobi. Then he had studied international law and human rights at a university in South Carolina, followed by an LL M in criminal law from the University of Teramo in Rome. He had done all this

62

with the aid of fellowships. While in Rome, he had been offered a job in New York and another in The Hague, but he had declined them because he wanted to come back home for reasons he now deemed incongruous, even foolishly nostalgic. He had met some Kenyans in Rome who had told him that he was mad to want to go back. Everything was going down the drain, they told him, including the coffee industry. Coffee plantations in many areas had been abandoned, they said, and were as yellow as dandelions in their state of neglect. The women and young boys who had once picked their ripe berries with laughter would now beat you up if you talked about coffee.

As Irwin lay in bed now, he supposed that he had come back because he had not entirely lost all hope. He had been looking for a job for the past year before the car crash that landed him in this hospital. But now that he was in this pain-ridden trap and with no more savings in his bank, he recognised that he had been mad, indeed, to come back. He was in a fleapit and with no means to lift himself out of it. It was for this realisation that he needed medication and not so much for his accident wounds, he knew.

He was thinking about this and considering the possibility of crying like some of the other men in the ward did every once in a while when his sister, Rima, arrived. He watched her as she hesitated at the entrance where the green ward doors were flung open, hit by the smell of sick men and hospital disinfectant. After so many years of being out under the sun on the sandy floor of the Turkwell Gorge he knew the smells of the hospital must have been particularly offensive to her. She walked down the aisle without looking at the sick men on either side or at the mustard-coloured walls, whose paint was peeling off in tiny flakes.

'I brought you some chicken broth and fruit salad,' she said when she reached his bed.

'I only asked for kale, Rima,' Irwin said, pulling himself up despite the fact that it hurt. Rima was an archaeologist in Turkwell Gorge, a largely dry ravine crawling up the furthest northern border of the country, where she lived in a tent and dug up fossils for the National Museums. They did not pay her much for what she did, and he knew that she had taken out an advance to come see him at this hospital in their hometown. Every time he looked into her face she seemed to have more fine lines descending the corners of her eyes. At thirty-two she was two years younger than he was, but it seemed to Irwin that she had outgrown him. He used to tell himself it was the sun in Turkwell Gorge, but the more he watched her, the more he was sure that it was because she no longer saw what was on the earth, but what was inside it. It was crazy to think as he did, but there were times he felt that she was as old as the very earth she dug.

She set the plastic dishes on the bedside stand next to the hospital porridge, which had set into a cold white mass in its bowl. 'I brought kale, too,' she said and opened the dish.

'I can feed myself,' he said when she proffered a spoonful. He tried to do so, but his hand trembled from weakness and banged against the dish as it came down from his mouth. The spoon fell on the bedsheet gathered at his waist and for a moment he wished the old nurse had not detached him from his IV cord from which he had drawn his sustenance without being humiliated like this. He did not reproach Rima when she picked up the spoon the second time around and resumed feeding him. He swallowed carefully, the food hurting his throat all the way down, and let the men watch him as he had watched them being fed by their women—kind mothers, wives, girlfriends, daughters and sisters. The young nurse sometimes fed the sick boy in the bed opposite his, across the aisle. The boy would lie there like a nestling, his mouth wide open, and swallow as fast as she shoved. He would then hold his puke till she was well done and gone for fear she would not bother to come by his bed again.

The doctor emerged from the tearoom. He was about to leave the ward when he turned and saw Rima. Irwin watched him as he stalled, said something to the old nurse who was seated behind the nurse station, and then looked at the charts of the two men with malaria who were sharing a bed. One of the men had cerebral malaria and sometimes screamed in the middle of the night. The doctor jammed his hands into his stark white coat and proceeded down the aisle. The coat made him seem more dark-skinned than he actually was. The features on his face were strongly chiselled and regal.

'Rima?' he said. 'Rima Labo?'

Rima looked up startled. Irwin watched her stare at the doctor for a while as she tried to remember where she might have met him.

The doctor smiled and said, 'It's me. Horace. Horace Moset. We went to mission school together. Same class.'

'Oh … *yes.* Horace,' Rima said, smoothing her khaki pants as she stood, and proffered a hand. 'Pardon me. You've changed so. This is my brother, Irwin.'

Irwin looked away, but could feel Horace's eyes on him. Irwin had long recognised the doctor; he had been one class ahead of the doctor and Rima in the Catholic mission school they had all attended in their childhood years, but had not bothered to introduce himself because it angered him that the doctor and the nurses could bring the little white tearoom down with laughter in the midst of all this sickness.

'You've hardly changed yourself, Rima,' Horace said, a smile in his voice.

Irwin supposed that was true, if Horace was assessing her physique. When they had been in mission school she had a very straight figure so that she looked like a walking ruler in that blue mission girl's uniform. Her figure had hardly filled out even now as she stood there in khaki and a white shirt rolled at the

65

sleeves. She hardly wore anything but khakis since she had started working up north.

'Horace Moset …' Rima said. 'I never fancied you a doctor.'

'I went to medical school in Gujarat,' he said.

Irwin scowled. Listening to them talk drove him round the bend. Medical school in *Gujarat*, he mused. India was as good a place to attend medical school as any, of course, but most of the students who went there were the ones who had been denied access into the public medical school in Nairobi. From what Irwin could remember of young Horace in mission school, it seemed he had been denied access to pretty much everything, including any academic club of significance. And now here he was, looking swanky and muttering sweet nothings to nurses so that they laughed like crass women in the marketplace. Irwin reckoned his slow recovery could well be attributed to malpractice and general incompetence, not to mention absolutely bad brains. Rima, obviously, thought very differently of this simpleton. She was the kind to say that it was the heart and not the mind that made a good doctor, much as Irwin would beg to differ.

'Well,' Irwin heard Horace say to Rima, at last, 'I'd better be getting along and let you get on with your lunch thing. Irwin is getting better. I could get him a wheelchair if you like. That way you can take him for a stroll next time.'

Next time Horace chose to chat up Rima, Irwin swore to himself, he would smear the man's face with verbal ordure. But it was three days before Rima showed up at the hospital again, and during that time Horace never came any closer than reading the chart at the end of his bed and asking a few innocuous questions to which Irwin grunted incomprehensible answers. An orderly brought a wheelchair around the afternoon Rima arrived. She had been typing up a report for the National Museums from her journals, she told him, as if to explain her absence. Irwin thought she had been merely angry at him for his obvious scowling at Horace, but did not want to counter her claim here in the ward before all the sick men.

The old nurse and the young nurse put him in the wheelchair and told her that she could wheel him about the hospital grounds for a short while. There was a small green at the end of the shaded corridors, which joined one ward to the next, and that is where they went. A stunted form of grass grew on it, and craggy bougainvillea stems crawled up the chain link fence. There was a gaping hole in the fence, and they saw a woman pushing her way in. Lots of people coming to visit their sick did that, Irwin guessed, watching the woman disentangle the hem of her large dress from ends of broken wire. The hospital had very strict visiting hours, which were few and far between and only allowed visitors at specific times. It seemed to Irwin that Rima visited at whatever hour she fancied, like now for instance, but he did not have the heart to ask if she came through the same hole or past the guard at the gate who had to be bribed to permit passage when it was not visiting hours. It was then that Irwin decided he was going to run over that guard's feet with his wheelchair and grind his toes into smithereens if he ever got the chance.

To distract himself from thinking about the guard he stared at the view the green presented. They were up on the hill, and the rest of the town spread out beneath them in dusty rooftops and a shimmering of mirages. There were some good and expensive clinics down there run by wealthy doctors who no longer worked up here on the hill.

As Irwin looked down the hill and then about himself, he realised that he had never really taken in this hill before, even though he had been born and raised in this town. Most of the people he had known in the town below never seemed to have much business up here. A prison stood across the dusty road opposite the hospital. Sewage ponds glittered between the long, untended grass; they were green from the algae blooming within. Verdant patches of cabbage and kale prospered beside the sewage ponds. There was a lot of kale in the prison compound and Irwin wondered how many prisoners it held within its fence. Kale and *sima*, a kind of maize flour cake, were staple foods in all public institutions like the prison and the hospital. Irwin had eaten a lot of kale in the public high school and public college he had attended away from his hometown in Nairobi. There were many things he did not like about those places, but he had liked the kale and still did.

'I suppose you know that you are quite rude for a helpless patient, Irwin,' Rima said. She had sat on the grass beside the wheel chair with her legs pulled up.

'I hate pretentious doctors, you know that. I had a medic for a roommate in Nairobi, remember?' Irwin was scowling and it made his head ache. 'They are all howlers in medical school. I bet Horace used to howl all the way from Gujarat to New Delhi. In college all the medical students would go drinking after their exams and come howling their way into the dorms at night like werewolves. He was a *howler*, I tell you. I wonder what the Gujarati word for howler is.'

Rima cast her eyes on the dusty rooftops of the town below and said nothing.

Irwin could not begin to understand why she was standing up for Horace like this; she was acting as if he was a mutual friend they had sold down the river, and he hated that. The sun made his eyes water, and he had to squint to properly visualise the prisoners tending the vegetable patches. They were in dirty white shirts and shorts. The ones in cleaner uniforms were barefoot while the ones in older, dirtier uniforms wore sandals like an emblem of their higher status. The sandals, *kalas* as they were known, were made from weathered tyre treads. *Kalas* were hard on one's feet, but they were cheap and lasted for a long time. Irwin knew that because every boy around here, his social status notwithstanding, tried on *kalas*. The *kala*-clad prisoners worked the vegetable patches with sharp metal *pangas*, while their barefoot compatriots had to pull out the weeds with their bare hands. A prison warden in green military fatigues watched over them, a bulky rifle slung over one shoulder. The prison chain-link fence, like the hospital's, had big holes in it, and it occurred to Irwin that the prisoners could easily overpower that one guard, whose rifle looked like it had to be reloaded after every shot like a goddamned musket.

'The thing with medics,' Irwin said slowly, 'is that they think they study the hardest thing in the world. Engineering students study the hardest, or architects. You remember architecture students in college, don't you, Rima? They sleep in the studio ... they live in the studio. Or take those guys doing nuclear science and double maths. Now, those are the real brain crackers, not medics. Medics are just howlers.'

His anger made his eyes water some more so that when he finally looked up the hill, he saw the cathedral through bleary eyes. The cathedral was built of quarried yellow stone and it raised a belled spire high up into the clear blue sky. Irwin stared at the cathedral until his tears receded. It was then that it hit him that there was a prison, a hospital and a cathedral up on the hill, in that order, all three of them raised high up here like Moses' bronze snake. This had never dawned on him before, and he wondered if Rima had noticed it.

Irwin had thought he was through with blood transfusions, but Horace had given him another that morning and now his body was very cold even though it was midday and hot inside the ward. Irwin thought he might be coming down with a fever and tried to fight it off with his mind, but he could hardly concentrate his entire willpower against it because he was pondering on the thought of a prison, a hospital and a cathedral being up here on the hill.

Sometimes, in the grapple of this deep chill from within, he thought the hospital was purgatory, the prison hell and the cathedral heaven. He must have already been thinking and dreaming these very same thoughts the evening before, because he had awoke to find the old nurse and the young nurse on either side of his bed, and all the sick men in the ward seated upright, staring at him. He must have been screaming like the man with cerebral malaria. He had been unable to go back to sleep until he saw the first beams of sunlight breaking through the gauzed windows.

As he pulled the linen sheet closer about himself, he noticed there was a priest in the ward. Irwin had seen him many times; he was always anointing the sick men or offering them the Eucharist. Whenever Irwin saw him headed his way he would close his eyes and pretend to be asleep. The priest was now holding the hand of the man who had AIDS. The man was very thin and had hollow, sunken eyes. Most of his hair had dropped off and the little that remained on his head had turned silky, like that of a newborn's. The man was crying like a widow, and all the sick men in the ward could hear him.

The young nurse was reading *Harper's Bazaar*. She was holding it very high to her eyes, and Irwin could see the glossy cover from where he lay. The old nurse was knitting. When the sick man stopped crying, he told the priest that he had slept with a lot of women in the shanty bars in town. Then he said that he had sold the family farm and squandered the money on himself and these other women, and his wife knew nothing of the matter. He also slept with his wife during the period he had slept with the other women and was afraid that he had passed on the disease to her. His voice was full of snot when he told the priest this. Irwin had seen the man's wife. She was almost as thin as he, and when she came into the ward to feed her husband, all the sick men in the ward watched her. Soon, the man started crying again. The priest sat on his bed and let him cry on his shoulder. When he was finally done crying, the priest suggested that he say the act of contrition and talk to his wife about the matter.

As the priest rose from the man's bed, he turned and caught Irwin's gaze. Irwin would have closed his eyes if it had not been too late. He hated the priest for making grown men cry. In particular, he hated him for that white collar, which loosened guilt within the men like expectorant loosened phlegm from the innermost recesses of one's lungs. Something happened to these men's eyes whenever the priest entered the ward. *Son of David*, they seemed to cry out in their pathetic silence, *have mercy on us!*

Now, as the priest walked over in his faded grey slacks and a yellow shirt wet on the shoulder, Irwin considered how he might altogether avoid talking to him. He hoped the priest would look at the information recorded on his chart at the end of the bed and leave him alone. At the bottom of each chart there was a slot marked religion under which were a series of denominations and corresponding empty boxes to tick according to the religion of the patient: Catholic, Protestant, Muslim and Other, they read. It was important to know the religion of each patient the old nurse had informed Irwin. The Muslims, she explained, had to be buried the very day they died. Irwin had told the old nurse that that was the most logical thing he had heard in a long time and that, if he should die, he would like to be buried immediately. The old nurse had put a mark beside 'Other.'

'Would you like me to hear your confession?' the priest asked Irwin, staring at his chart.

'I have nothing to confess,' Irwin replied, wondering whether the priest could not read a word as simple as 'Other.' If there was one thing Irwin did not want, it was to cry. He simply would not.

'Is there anything else I can do for you then—anything at all?' The priest looked at the wheelchair, which was folded up against the wall and back at Irwin.

71

Irwin was sore from having to lie down for so long. A little direct sunshine, he thought, would make him feel better. 'I would be delighted,' Irwin told the priest, 'if you could wheel me out for a few minutes.'

The priest opened up the wheelchair. Then he half bent over Irwin, offering him the breadth of his shoulders to hold onto as his arms slipped under, lifting him off the bed and onto the chair. The priest's arms felt very strong and Irwin's lips trembled because he realised he had lost a lot of weight. He did not feel this bad when that old matriarch of a nurse lifted him or turned him on the bed because he liked to think she had the strength of a bull and could just as easily have lifted a house.

'Where would you like to go?' the priest asked.

'Anywhere,' Irwin replied.

They went to the green where he always went with Rima. The priest sat beside the wheelchair, pulled up his legs like Rima did, and looped his long arms over his bent knees. 'Do you work?' he asked.

'Nobody will hire me, here,' Irwin said. He lifted his face to the sun and closed his eyes as the warmth slowly spread through him. 'I've sent out more applications than I care to remember, but all I get are rejections. They say I'm overqualified, or else they just need a simple lawyer … some licensed idiot, not me.'

The priest chuckled. 'A lawyer …' he mused.

'This country has gone to the dogs,' Irwin swore.

'When you're up on this hill,' the priest said, 'you should think of the most beautiful place you've been. What's the most beautiful place you've been?'

Irwin leaned further back into his wheelchair. 'Rome,' he murmured.

'You've been to Rome?' the priest asked, his voice intent with curiosity.

'Yes. I studied in Rome.'

'Tell me that the Vatican City is as beautiful as I have heard it is.'

'I never went to Vatican City,' Irwin said.

'You've been to Rome and never went to the Vatican?' the priest asked very slowly.

'Yes, that's right.'

'Not even once—to pray?'

'No.'

The priest was quiet for a long time. 'You don't believe in prayer, do you?'

Irwin sat up straight and opened his eyes. 'No.'

Across in the prison Irwin noticed a man in a white coat emerge from one of the baked mud buildings holding a small bundle in his arms. Then a guard, with a rifle slung over one shoulder, emerged from the same building and after him the figure of a woman in a pinkish gown. The woman stumbled about and clung to the man with the white coat. The guard seized her by the arm and dragged her away. After a while he gave up on dragging her and lifted her into his arms and they both disappeared into the warren of prison buildings.

The man in the white coat walked through the vegetable patches, circled the sewers to where there was a hole in the fence and squeezed through carefully, protecting the bundle in his arms under the curve of his chest. As the man walked closer Irwin saw that it was Horace.

'What is he carrying?' Irwin asked the priest.

'A baby,' the priest replied. 'He's a good man, the doctor. He does things he doesn't have to.'

'Where is he going to take it?' Irwin asked, still puzzled, even though it occurred to him that a prison was not the best of places for a newborn.

'To the children's ward; for a couple of weeks at least. If the woman's relatives don't come for it then, the nurses will turn the

73

baby over to me, and I will turn it over to the mission orphanage.'

Irwin stared at the road that led up to the cathedral. Horace was a good man, the priest had said, a good man doing things he does not have to be doing, and Irwin knew that he could not counter that up here on the hill any longer after what he had witnessed. So he studied the road and its yellow dust and the abundance of broken rock strewn on its uneven shoulders. In Rome, Irwin had seen an old painting of the *Via Dolorosa*, the road that Jesus had taken on his way to Golgotha. The road to the cathedral looked very much like the old *Via Dolorosa* even though he had traversed the modern *Via Dolorosa* itself in Rome and drank mocha coffee in one of it sidewalk cafes.

'If I prayed and you got a job, would you believe in the power of prayer?' the priest asked.

'I will not get a job. Not here,' Irwin said.

'What if I pray and you get one?' the priest insisted.

Irwin was looking at the road. It was very hot and those stones looked very sharp. 'If you pray and I get a job,' Irwin said, 'I will walk up the hill to your great cathedral with only my shirt on. No shoes, no pants, no nothing. Just my shirt. How about that?'

When the priest heard this, he reeled on the grass and laughed very hard. Irwin looked at him as he laughed. He laughed so hard that Irwin, in the end, laughed too. This priest was very handsome. He was very tall and very lean and very brown and when he laughed, his smile was very deep. He had nice hands with long fingers. His fingernails were clean and clipped. His hairline was receding and he was clean-shaven, but he was very handsome nonetheless. And true to God, out there on the green that afternoon, Irwin thought that he looked like an angel.

It was Rima who brought him the letters three weeks afterwards. By then Irwin had forgotten how hard he had laughed with the priest that afternoon because things seemed to have gone from bad to worse in the ward. The old man who looked like a bird in really bad shape no longer made his daily pilgrimage to the toilets. It happened that one time he had gone down to the toilets, but nobody had heard anything come out. The old nurse and the young nurse had fitted him with a catheter and that was that.

The man with cerebral malaria had screamed so violently one night that the nurses had taken him into the ICU. He had not returned since and nobody had asked after him because he could not possibly be in the ICU anymore. The man with AIDS had simply gone to sleep one night and failed to wake up the following morning. Only the boy who puked seemed to have made any real progress. He could eat his meals on his own now and had gained some weight. However, he could not leave the ward because his bills were not yet paid. Thus he whiled the day away looking out of the window. Irwin had decided that he would help the poor boy leave. There is a hole in the fence—this is what he would tell the boy.

So it was after Rima had left the dread of the ward and Irwin had read the letters that he remembered how hard he and the priest had laughed and what each had staked. There were two job acceptance letters. One offered him a position at the prestigious law firm, Scot & Morrison, in Nairobi. Scot & Morrison was one of the first firms he had applied for a job; they had clients like Citibank Nairobi, and litigated some of the most prominent cases in the country. The other was from the International Criminal Tribunal for Rwanda in Arusha. The international court was offering him a position as defence counsel for Rwandan genocide suspects who could not afford a lawyer of their own. This great court lying under the shadow of Mt Kilimanjaro wanted him, Irwin Labo, to defend a group of desperados; men who lay rotting in the UN jails of Arusha like the sick men in this ward.

He folded the letters carefully and returned them to their envelopes before leaning against the steel bar at the head of the bed. Horace walked into the ward to do his rounds. Irwin watched him as he came down the aisle slowly, reading footboard charts and asking the usual questions. 'I never, in my wildest dreams, imagined Rima an archaeologist,' he said, when he reached Irwin's bed.

'It suits her,' Irwin said with a shrug. It was the first time he had acknowledged so himself. Rima Labo could not be anything but an archaeologist digging the earth. 'She likes looking for early man.'

'Early man. Well, I'll be damned,' Horace said, shaking his head with a smile. 'Early man was—'

'Early man was a nutcracker … a *Zinjanthropus*,' Irwin said. 'He was simple and there was nothing on his hills but trees.'

Horace laughed. It occurred to Irwin that Horace had a laugh somewhat similar to the priest's. That priest could laugh the dead awake. He reminded Irwin of how he and Rima once used to laugh over nothing. As Irwin watched Horace he found that he could not recall exactly when or where the laughter had faded within him.

'What are you going to do when you leave this place?' Horace asked.

'I don't know,' Irwin said. 'Look for another rat hole?'

'You're not going bonkers, are you?' Horace asked.

Irwin laughed at the question. He liked laughing like this, he realised, among the desperados. It felt like he was definitely headed for another rat hole. 'Not quite,' he replied. 'If you'll excuse me now, I'd like to take a walk.'

As Irwin Labo wriggled out of his pyjama bottoms under the sheets he already saw himself up on the very peak of the hill collapsing from the effort and pain of it all, and the throttle of suppressed laughter. He and the priest would laugh, he knew, as they had on the green.

THE ZOROASTRIAN PHOTOGRAPHER

This is a story about the photographs Sanjar Atash took while on a train journey to the Chinvat Bridge at the age of twenty-six. He kept the photos he took on that surreal train to himself throughout his career. They were faded black-and-white prints he would finally give to me, his only child and daughter, many years later before he died; to be exact, it was only a month before I gave up his body to the vultures that fly on high as he had willed and as Parsi Zoroastrian custom has always willed even for its Diaspora this far off in East Africa. The prints had been preserved in an old copy of Rabindranath Tagore's *Atithi*—O how he loved that young Brahmin wanderer, Tarapada. Alas, he was Tarapada himself!

So easy to wander like my own father, like Tarapada—that restless itinerant who would not stay at home with his folk or marry a tax collector's daughter, but back we go to the train my father was on. All he had abruptly and inexplicably wished for on that train journey, he had told me, was sleep; it, however, had evaded him. Whenever he tried to close his eyes and sink into sleep's soothing embrace, he would soon after awaken to the sound of a vulture screeching in his head—vultures, vultures, vultures, he had told me, as he lay in a sisal hammock between two umbrella thorn trees in our Kenyan Rift Valley home in Eldoret, facing the very red brick mansion he had built over his parents' demolished iron sheet canteen.

'Vultures, my dear Royaa,' he had told me, the sky reflected in his eyes, 'Vultures every waking hour! I was between life and death, like the vulture, which flies between the earth and the heavens.'

Tormented by the vulture, which flies higher than any other bird, he had concluded that some vodka might help. He had a bottle in his Revelation Expandable 1940s suitcase. The vodka was made from the finest Stobrawa potatoes; it was luxury potato vodka he had once bought in Landi Kotal.

'All the way from Krakow's black market to Landi Kotal, where it is forbidden,' he had mused about the vodka aloud, swinging in the hammock, back and forth, back and forth, all the while knowing that the vulture would soon be flying over his *dakhma* and his sickly body would presently be a lifeless body simply lying there waiting for the vulture's hungry descent. He had already felt the imminence of death last April when the rains had begun and Eldoret was moss green and my mother, sick with worry, was saying it was about time that I got married. My mother wanted to secure the future, while my father wanted to secure the past.

'Your mother thinks that I took these old photos when I was on the Khyber train to Landi Kotal,' he had told me, 'but she is wrong.'

'But why speak of Landi Kotal, so far from home?' I had asked.

'Why speak of Landi Kotal, Royaa?' he had returned as if surprised by the question. 'Why speak of the moon? Why speak of the stars? Why speak of union with your *fravashi*? Why speak of the final cosmic renovation? Landi Kotal was about going the farthest I could. In that smugglers' town, one could get the latest kind of machine gun to the choicest Oudh perfume. But that is not where I was headed when I took these old photos.'

Listening to him speak, I could not help but marvel at the exquisite nose my father had for scents. My mother and I had an assortment of perfumes from all the places he passed through taking photos. But back to the potato vodka, which did not help in what he liked to alternatively refer to as his hour of need or his tormenting moment of spiritual individuation when he took these overexposed and out-of-focus photos that were really no good. Bearing in mind the delicate nature of both the past and present circumstances, however, I did not have the heart to comment about the quality of these particular photos because there were so many great ones that he had shot before and, *especially*, after his train journey to the Chinvat Bridge. So I could only listen to him reminisce about how he had sat red-eyed in his train cabin until he smashed the vodka bottle against the wall in frustration. He relished the sound of breaking glass scattering about as delicate as tinkle bell sounds on a girl's *ghungharu*. He had a vision then, he said, of a hot desert in Pakistan, endless shimmering mirages of it; he was on a winding track leading to Nagar Parkar, where his grandparents had once lived, where the houses nestled close to each other hyperventilating—granite tiles baking on the roofs and sandstone walls burnt golden brown by the desert heat.

He told me that he had been looking for an ancient Zoroastrian Fire Temple to photograph in the land of his ancestors; it was a lost temple centuries old. But he could not seem to find it in Nagar Parkar and so he moved on to Sardhara despite the bleeder heat wave. But all he found there was a Hindu Mahadeve temple in ruins waiting to be rebuilt yet again. In his vision, across time, he stood there studying the worn surface of the temple steps, which led to a dilapidated main hallway. Wind abrasion had turned the steps into a *zeugen* scape of tiny ridges and furrows. He set his camera on a tripod under the shade of a petrified tree close by, screwed on his zoom lens, and then circled the temple, studying the steps, looking for an interesting perspective, considering every angle, knowing that he had to envision the photo in his mind before he could even take it. The Hindu river temples he had seen before always seemed to have leaf litter on their steps, the scent of Jasmine and Vinca in the air, and ancient banyan trees set on lawns of Mondo grass for pilgrims to sit under and meditate. Once, in the Hindu temples dotting the Ghat of Varanasi, he had seen nothing but pilgrims. In this sacked desert temple, however, there was no leaf litter and there were no pilgrims. The seasonal stream had dried and the holy pond was drying. On these hot steps of the Mahadeve temple was nothing but shifting sands under the whims of a wild wind, an open desert sky, and no sign of a rain squall that might bring relief. This was the scene that my father shot: a fallen temple awaiting the attentions of the Sompuras, master masons of Gujarat. And then it was all gone, like a spectre, this holy vision, and now he had nothing to show for it but an old blurry photo whose original composition he could only conjure up with words.

This is how I remember him: father at sixty swinging in his hammock, while I idly collected the umbrella tree pods scattered on the grass. I would have them ground in the local mill and then use them to garnish wheat flour for our chapattis. This is what I had thought about at the time, chapattis, and not the preparations my mother was making to transport him to an old Parsi guesthouse in Karachi, where he would eventually die and his linen-shrouded body carried to a close by Dakhma for a sky burial. It would be his last act of charity, to let the vultures have what would otherwise be corrupted and turn it into a living energy.

'Perhaps it is best to leave the past alone and not obsess about the photos,' I had eventually said to him.

'Leave the past alone, Royaa?' he had asked with a chuckle. 'One does not need to tell the child of a hyena to limp.'

Ah, yes, his past, my past, our past, was Parsi. But being Parsi was also our present and future—just as the hyena limps, and his children limp, and so on and so forth. His beard had grown long and peppered and his dark eyes were turning milky. So I let him continue with his story on that mysterious train and how he had left his cabin and ventured into the dining area. There was a Swahili man seated there in a white suit and a white *kofia* on his hennaed head and a white ivory walking cane against one leg.

'Four things are too wonderful for me; four I do not understand,' he was saying. 'The way of a vulture in the sky, the way of an old serpent on a rock, the way of a maiden with a man, and the way of a train to the Chinvat Bridge.'

Sanjar Atash was glad that he had come here and met this wise Swahili man. 'I haven't been well,' he told him. 'I feel sick, lost, like I am alone …'

'In a land of a thousand fields,' the man completed his sentence.

'Yes,' he replied slowly, thinking over the strange phrase. 'Perhaps I need to see a doctor.'

'Perhaps,' the man said.

'Or maybe I just need to eat and sleep.'

'Eat and sleep. Sounds like a great idea,' the man said as he offered him his dessert, a slice of black forest cake.

Sanjar wanted a piece of the cake, but its sweet smell nauseated him.

'Well,' the man said, 'perhaps my pet will have it.'

It was then that my father saw it, the man's pet, a great African White-Backed Vulture, *Gyps africanus*, perched on a chair at the end of the dining cabin. Its strong-beaked head moved from side to side, an eager appendage on a long naked neck that allowed it to delve deep into animal and human flesh, deep enough to get to the soft tissues and intestines, which it relished. It could gobble down close to three pounds of flesh in under five minutes. Now, this Old World creature, this strict meat-eater, was consuming a piece of black forest cake, pecking at it, head bobbing up and down, black beak covered in warm chocolate.

'My vulture lost his ability to fly,' the man said. 'Power lines … they are everywhere these days.'

My father nodded, speechless; his camera was suddenly as heavy as a ship's anchor around his neck.

'You mustn't look so miserable,' the man said.

'It must be the cold in here,' he replied. 'Do you feel it?'

81

'Have some *chai*,' the Swahili man in a white suit said, pouring him a cup.

The tea was milky and sweet and tasted of *Nuskhe* spices. Eldoret tea mixed with Pakistani *Nuskhe* spices.

'Would you like to hear a story about how Manx cats lost their tails?' the man asked. 'I have a Manx cat that I bought from an English tourist in Mombasa. He was an old man, this tourist. As old as the oldest door in England, he had joked before telling me the Manx-cat story … a tale from his country. You've not heard the story before, have you?'

'No, I haven't,' my father answered, sipping the *chai*, his hands cupping the china for warmth as he tried to ignore the man's pet vulture and concentrate on his Manx-cat story.

'Well,' the man said, 'here is Noah, all hustled and busy calling in the animals into his ship because the flood is coming. And the cat, you won't believe it, is still out there looking for a mouse or something stupid like that. Now, Noah gets impatient and annoyed and threatens to shut the cat out.'

According to my father, the Swahili man had paused at that juncture, looked deep into his eyes and said with a very solemn voice: '*Yes*, that cat was going to be shut out altogether! And Noah slams the door just as the cat is running in. Wham! And the poor cat's tail is a goner', He snapped his fingers loudly. 'Yeah, just like that, and Noah doesn't care a sod.'

And Noah doesn't care a sod—the words, my father said to me, could not seem to leave his mind even after he left the Swahili man and his vulture and was back again in his cabin. It had begun to rain and he was now wavering in between sleep and consciousness. *And Noah doesn't care a sod.* It had not been good to see the vulture, which reminded him of a sky burial he had not yet reconciled himself to. *And Noah doesn't care a sod.* But the *chai* had helped. *And Noah doesn't care a sod.* The sodding Manx-cat story had deflated any good feelings induced by the *chai*. *And Noah doesn't care a sod.* And then he had made it worse by photographing the vulture because it had fluttered on its damaged wings when the flash went off and had fallen off the chair. *And Noah doesn't care a sod.*

He had devoted his entire mind to the business of falling asleep; unfortunately, he found himself in merely another vision, this time at his parents' canteen in Eldoret. He had always felt cramped in that little four-walled contraption where he had grown up selling sugar, kerosene, sliced bread from Nairobi, ghee, maize flour, Pepsi-cola, matches, thread …

'Interest, Sanjar,' his own father was saying in Urdu, 'is like a racing horse: here today, gone tomorrow.'

Unfortunately, he had said the same thing about his first camera, a Polaroid. How many years ago was that? 'I saved up some money for a Nikon, and I'm now taking some really good pictures, Papi,' Sanjar had said to his father. 'These are the ones. I feel it in my bones.'

'Really?' his mother asked from one corner of the canteen. She was making *paratha*—fried bread and eggs, together with some lentil stew for dinner.

'*Accha,*' Sanjar replied. His mother was always hoping that he would make a big killing out of his photos and have enough money to marry and raise a family. 'Yes, I think these will get me an exhibition in Nairobi.'

'Photos, photos, photos …' his father moaned as he sat cross-legged on a straw mat holding his head in his hands, the lines on his face visible even under the weak kerosene lamp. He used the same chastening voice his teachers had once used on him at the BVS Parsi High School in Karachi. 'These photographs will get you nowhere, Sanjar. Do you not know that this canteen is better than a camera? And that a wife is better than a camera as well?'

'I am happy enough with my camera and my photographs.'

83

'Sometimes I think you are a coward,' his father had said, 'A coward, who refuses to fully participate in life!'

'I'm no coward!' Sanjar retorted. 'Tell him that I'm not, Mama.'

But his mother had her veiled head bowed and her eyes cast away. 'Good thoughts, good words, good deeds … that is what really matters, Sanjar,' she had said and continued turning the frying bread on the pan.

'I am not a coward,' Sanjar repeated in a weak, breathless, and confounded whisper.

His father reached into the shadows and retrieved a copy of the weekly *Akhbar-e-Jehan*, which a cousin still faithfully mailed him from Karachi. He began to read it and would not respond to Sanjar.

In an effort to elicit support from another quarter, Sanjar turned to their house help, who was tinkering with the cassette player. He was a tall wiry Masai, who used to walk him to school when he was just a boy. His name was Legishon—the polite one. Legishon, with his braided ochre-coloured hair and the smell of sour milk thick in his breath, never seemed to be afraid of anything. He was a man at ease with himself. He walked to the rhythm of his iron foot bells and planted his sandals firmly on the dusty roads. He had confidence in the skill with which he wielded his spear and the sounds his ears trapped. He still wore the steel bangles his grandfather had forged after raiding the Kenya–Uganda railway during its construction as it had crossed tribal land under British conquest. Legishon was now standing on one leg with the other bent at the knee, a classic Masai yoga-like pose anchored by a walking stick, as though he were still pasturing cattle out there in the savannah.

'I am not a coward,' Sanjar repeated, staring at him, willing him to come to his aid.

'The mouth of a camel, Sanjar, is not afraid of thorns,'

Legishon said and went back to tinkering with the cassette player.

Jean-Philippe Rameau's opera *Zoroastre* blared from the speakers, and suddenly Sanjar Atash found himself jolted back into his former vision in the train cabin; he was seated on his wall bed, eyes wide open, sweat having soaked right through his white cotton *Sedrah*, his heart pounding.

Here, he once more found himself haunted by the sombre voice of the Swahili man, who had a pet vulture, as he said: 'I was standing in the sun when I saw the Chinvat Bridge narrowing for the wicked soul. There was nowhere for the wicked soul to turn when the demon Vizaresh appeared to drag it into the House of Lies. Have you examined your soul, Sanjar Atash? Have you considered what will happen to it when the Daevas cut off your eyesight at the end of your days? Will the Chinvat Bridge widen for you? Will the beautiful maid and her dogs lead you into the House of Song?'

'Death was there with me on that train, Royaa,' my father had said to me. 'Out there in the corridor was the unmistakable sound of his timeless steps, slow, unhurried, certain of their destination, and so heavy I felt the floorboards in my cabin warp to breaking point. Death was there cajoling me out of my body, out of the train, out of Eldoret, out of the Rift Valley, and across the Indian Ocean to Karachi ... high up in the forested hills above Karachi's skyline where the open-air *dakhmas* are built. It was my fate; what a faithful Parsi ought to hope for—to let the vulture have the body and set the soul free for that bountiful reward at the head of the Chinvat Bridge. Ah, the mouth of a camel is not afraid of thorns, Royaa!

'Better to go the way of the sky than the way of the earth, I had said to myself. Better the vulture than the worms. Better a few hours with the vulture than a century with the worms. Better the vulture, which soars through the skies with my flesh. Better the vulture to lead me to my *Uru* than the worms. Death was to be

85

embraced, I had been taught from birth. *Khush Amdid*—welcome, to my very body, I should say to it. The vulture's beak and the vulture's talons were the gateway to what lay beyond life. My eyes for the vulture, my nose for the vulture, I should now vow and be forever free, I had thought to myself. Tonight I say *Khush Amdid* to the darkness beyond, which has its eyes set on me.

'And so I rose from my bed and set my feet on the floor. Death, *of course*, heard! He heard for he came to a stop and with him his flock of vultures with their slow, unmistakable wing beat. I listened to those wings as they slowed their rhythm, each deathly beat a trifle slower than the other, until their talons touched upon my cabin's roof like a sudden burst of hailstones.

'Standing there barefoot, I lost control of my heart and the poor muscle pounded away like a war drum under giant mallets. Breath cringed away from me on its own accord, unwilling to be heard, and an unspeakable and ageless horror engulfed the precincts of my soul as I willed myself to take a photo of death, Royaa.'

But the steam whistle on the train had blasted through the night: Choooooo! Choooooo! Choooooo!

It shattered the momentary terror that had encased him, he had told me.

It was then that he had dashed for his cabin door before he could have the time to change his mind and flung it wide open, at last ready to meet death face to face. But instead of death, a hard gust of cold air and rain hit him right on his face and torso, and it took several minutes before he realised that it was morning and he was no longer on the train to the Chinvat Bridge but flying above Karachi in a vulture's body! It was Karachi for sure as spread out below him was the vast complex of Pakistani Steel slowly puffing up columns of hot steam and industrial smoke. This is where his father's cousin, the one who faithfully paid his subscription to a weekly copy of the *Akhbar-e-Jehan*, worked as an engineer. When he

86

had first gotten the job, he had sent out some photos of the place to Eldoret and later bought Sanjar his first camera, the Polaroid, as a birthday present. Wet and cold, but flying steadily on now, he could see the other men and women who worked with his father's cousin pouring in from Steel Town in their cars, and beyond that, in the Quaid-I-Azam Park, a few runners on the jogging track as it weaved past man-made lakes swarming with white water birds.

He had swooped down closer to the city taking photographs and slowly making his way beyond Pakistani Steel to downtown Karachi. Away from Steel Town, the port was a drenched and overcast concrete-scape with a deserted beach. The sweet and nimco shops were closed. Auto rickshaws studded the traffic, and the jam thickened as blaring horns, exhaust fumes, and impatience filled the air. He could tell who they were intuitively, those Parsi drivers and passengers who upon looking out of their car windows in the lunacy of the morning's traffic saw him and then hurriedly turned away in the face of their own final destiny: the vulture. *Ah*, those hyena's children that would not limp! Those camel mouths afraid of thorns! When he circled their cars in an attempt to get their attention once more, they merely buried their faces in the headline news of the *Daily Jang, Dawn, IQRA* or weekly *Akhbar-e-Jehan*. Fools—they are fools like I once was, he had thought, the camera swinging like a pendulum on his long, naked vulture neck. He had the vulture's prayer and it would be a blessing to them in the land of a thousand fields: this was the message he wanted to pass on. It was knowledge too wonderful.

I now swing on what used to be my father's sisal hammock between the two umbrella thorn trees with knowledge too wonderful. My mind wanders endlessly; like Father's, like Tarapada's. Yet it is a peaceful wandering where I am at ease with what I see: Legishon in his old age basking on the terrace; our dog, Jamal, a deep-brown Pakistani Sindh Mastiff, at Legishon's feet, gently waging his tail; Mama on a white garden chair talking on a cell phone I bought her and very much still on a mission to get me married; and then above us all the blue sky where the vulture soars. With knowledge too wonderful, I place my father's photographs back where they have always been: in Tagore's *Atithi*.

WHERE I HAVE COME FROM

People always said that my mother was a good woman. When some local men complimented her thus, they were mostly trying to win her hand in marriage, but when women themselves or children said 'a good woman you are, ——,' they actually meant it. Children could remember tripping and falling and my mother lifting them to her breast for inspection at the health clinic. They would show her their nettle rash and beg not to be injected. 'A sweet for your *siwot*,' she would say to them. 'No injections today.' While the women, the old ones especially, with daughters and sons working in the flower farms and tea estates, could remember her carrying their *kwenik* up one hill or the other and helping them start a fire in their homesteads. Old age is shared, she would always say arranging the firewood, growing up is good. So you see, if things were as they once were in this Kenyan Rift Valley town of Eldoret, I would tell you her name because there are those who would bless her in remembrance—all those children with accidental encounters with *chemelet*—the stinging creeper, malaria, coughs, and colds. Believe me, I would tell you her name. In the very least, I would divulge her porridge name, given at the moment of her birth, but we are all now like the chimpanzees which must live without tails.

Names simply do not come forth from people's lips easily these days. They do not wish to reveal their names and neither do they wish to hear yours. I would liken the name—my mother's, mine, and yours even—to the elephant which was killed by a devoted and systematic effort. Where I have come from, one's name could be their death for it usually points to one's ethnicity. When one wakes and bathes and eventually considers what to wear before the mirror, they consider their name as well. Names have turned into markers; they are our verbalised ethnic yellow stars distinguishing the outsider from the insider. No one is exempt from what the wrong name signifies, not even the Benedictine priests who founded the health clinic where my mother worked. Take Fr ____, who was the Vice Rector at the nearby seminary, for instance. He had studied at the Biblicum and would bake ciriola, traditional Roma bread, with his students every Saturday afternoon. I know this because it was common knowledge. Anyway, Fr ____ and his students woke one morning and found two families seated on the seminary lawn under the towering stone statue of St Anthony of Padua. They had the wrong names, all fourteen of them. Fr ____ invited them for morning Mass and for the first time in the history of the seminary's chapel there was the scent of women breastfeeding their babies in it. Fr ____ burnt incense scented with the various aromas of Sandalwood, Myrrh, Galangal and Sage. All the mystique of The Frankincense Trail filled the chapel, but would not overwhelm that of the women and their babies. Fr ____, still sleepy, was thinking of this and not God when the housekeeper interrupted Mass to tell him that there was a group of men demanding an audience with him. When Fr ____ went out to meet the men, he found them standing near the statue of St Anthony of Padua as well. They were carrying bow and arrows, *pangas* and big sticks, and smelt of smoke and human blood. Among them, Fr ____ recognised a man he had helped with school fees for his children; another, whose pregnant wife he had ferried to hospital; and the local councillor's son who was carrying a Kalashnikov. They were neighbours, familiar faces, demanding for people they knew from the same *koret* but with the 'wrong names.'

We do not choose our names or our tribes, Fr ____ explained. He felt, believed, that he could talk to them. *Sere!* (Be blessed!) he had greeted them.

They voted for the wrong party, the men said.

We live in a democracy, no? Fr ____ countered. We all vote

for who we like. My brothers, when two hippos quarrel you do not put your oar in.

They are thieves, the men said. They started singing war songs. They shook their warrior thigh-bells. They brandished their weapons in Fr ___'s face.

Women and children, you mean? Babies, old men and fathers who love their families? These are the people you want to kill?

If they are not for us, they are against us. The same goes for you, Father, you and your church.

You know, he told the councillor's son, the man who invented that gun, Mikhail Kalashnikov, was given an award that is in honor of St Andrew, the first apostle of Jesus.

So what?

This man claims that he sleeps well. That it's the politicians who are to blame for failing to come to an agreement and resorting to violence.

You only think that way because you are one of them!

They killed him right there under the shadow of St Anthony of Padua, patron saint of the amputated and the disenfranchised. And when they were done, they proceeded into the seminary. All this happened at the crack of dawn. Some residents of the town, those with the right names, were slowly rousing themselves from sleep, while those with the wrong names were getting ready for bed, having kept vigil all night. Yet others, in an effort to earn a living, ignored the full implications of their names and were already up loading roses, carnations and the red-brown berried hypericums, destined for Europe, into trucks. Those with the wrong names cut and packed these flowers while those with an acceptable name drove the truck for they would not be attacked.

Even the *boda boda* man (the bicycle taxi man) is aware of this fact—the complexity of the name—as it could be the difference between life and death for his passengers. The ideal *boda boda* man speaks many languages and has many names; he is like the chameleon which looks in all directions before moving. Such is the situation certain people have found themselves in where I come from. What shall I be called today? they ask themselves, these outsiders, looking away from their dressing mirrors and out the window (for those lucky few who have not yet been put out and their houses repainted by strangers) to the new high rise buildings of Eldoret Town and onward to Sergoit Hill, which still dominates the skyline. Who shall I be known as? Where should I hail from? Which of my many identity cards is most suitable? Alas, they find, like my own mother did, that the name has become part of their wardrobe. A name, a suitable name that is, covers up their perceived foreignness much like clothes cover up nakedness. Should they, as well, wash it, put it out to dry in the sun, and then iron it ready for wear? Even throw it away when it is no longer suitable?

That is how my mother began her days in those months before her death (our death I should really say), asking questions that are now ritually asked each morning by those who do not have the right names but have chosen to continue living here in a massive field of plastic refugee camp tents or abandoned, half-burnt buildings or in the still standing suburbs of Langas and Munyaka. She would put on her pressed sky-blue nurse's uniform, and my father would zip her up carefully, the floral scent of her perfume in his nose. He was not happy about her going to work pregnant with me, but he was hardly earning any money himself as this was his sophomore year at the Kip Keino Training Centre for track runners. He had enrolled at the centre after years of an unsuccessful road running regimen, which always clashed with his work as a supermarket cashier. He was going for the real deal, he told my mother: full-time training. He was devoted to running the marathon and qualifying for the Olympics at the national championships. So he accepted my mother working and watched with wonder as her stomach grew and her belly button popped and her underbelly skin stretched into a map-like semblance of the many rivers of the place we called home: ah, he would say, loving and laughter in his eyes, here is Kipkarren River, here is Mogong and Yala, and this surely must be Mtetei heading to Nyando, oh, look at Pire Swamp! She would smile, happy to be lying in his arms as exposed as a beached whale, and in turn would document the slow transformations of his marathon body, which she massaged every so often.

Such were the quiet moments of their private life. They would lock out the world to be alone in this place which was once dominated by the Wanderobo, and then the Sirkwa, and then the Nandi, and then white British and Afrikaans settlers before the arrival of people from all walks of life in independent Kenya.

Truth be told, we are a nation of migrants, travellers, and foreigners to a place we call home: ours. Fr ———, before dying, said as much to the men who were killing him: 'we're all foreigners on earth' were his last words.

Where I have come from, people have forgotten their own mortality. They sit beside their radios listening to ethnic FM stations and sharpen their hate for the likes of my mother and my father (because he had married a woman with the wrong name), and Fr ———: outsiders, they vow, will be pursued and killed even in their ancestral lands way across the Rift Valley. On the highways, outsiders are flushed from their vehicles. In universities and schools, outsiders are flushed from their dorms and classes.

What has befallen Eldoret can be likened to a slow, flesh-eating disease. Those who say it never used to be this way can only be compared to a naive sailor who does not recognise the signs of a coming storm. The storm had been gathering for years in Eldoret and the surrounding lands: what is happening in Eldoret had already happened in Kuresoi and Molo and Mt Elgon. Nothing, after all, is new under the sun.

There's a faint odour in the air now, where I come from. Sometimes the odour is merely a lingering memory easily mistaken for a reality by a traumatised mind, but sometimes it is an actual reenactment of what has passed. Either way, there it is, this odour, whiffing through the town, sometimes surpassing the milky smells of the Donyo Lessos Cheese Factory on Kenyatta Street, raising the hair on the back of peoples' necks as they walk past Will's Bar, snapping upright slouched backs in cyber cafes, turning emergency room heads at the Medical Town Campus, causing a sudden loss of appetite for a dinner at the Sirikwa Hotel, putting a stop to laughter among a group of tea pickers from Kaptein Tea Estate spending their weekend in town for they still remember forty of their own who fell to machetes. It is unshakeable, this odour. It comes from miles upon miles of dry corn ready for harvest burning; of smouldering tea plants, some sixty years of age, which have been smeared with the very blood of hands that have picked it; of burning houses—concrete crumbling with heat, soot-coated iron sheets buoyed up by hot air like Aladdin's mat, glass windows splintering in the inferno; and, among much more, the smell of my mother burning with me inside her.

When you hear that women and children were burnt alive while taking refuge at Kiambaa Church in Eldoret and then again at a house in Naivasha in an act of vengeance, remember I was among them. And when you hear that a marathon runner was also killed on his way home, remember that it was because he loved my mother. He was well prepared for it, this last marathon. Those who ran after him can attest to that. There were hundreds of them, some on foot, some on bicycles, some in lorries carrying sections of the railway line they had just vandalised, but he outran them all. When they realised that they would not catch him, one of them raised his bow and arrow and shot him down. Thus my father died as he had lived: running. In that last race, it was us that he was running for. *Sere!*